WHO KILLED THE STARLET?

THE TIGHTWAD PRODUCER
Mitchell Grafman, who was putting up the bucks to keep her in his bed?

THE HOSTILE WRITER
Sherman Ruskin, who *knew* she was all wrong for the part?

THE NERVOUS COMPOSER
Gary Webber, who needed a success to get his career going?

THE L.A. REWRITE MAN
Alvin Persky, who wanted more money than he was worth?

THE ECOLOGY ACTIVIST
Sarah McChesney, who wanted to thwart Thea's plans for building on the island?

THE MUSCLE-BOUND BOATMAN
Leroy, who couldn't stand it when women didn't want him?

C.B. GREENFIELD: THE PIANO BIRD

Lucille Kallen

BALLANTINE BOOKS • NEW YORK

Library of Congress Catalog Card Number: 83-43197

ISBN 0-345-31118-3

This edition published by arrangement with Random House, Inc.

Manufactured in the United States of America

First Ballantine Books Edition: February 1985

*For
Joan Probber,
that rare individual,
the perfect traveling companion*

*and for
Jeanne Dolgin,
who discovered Sanibel
long after Ponce de Léon*

ACKNOWLEDGMENTS

A number of people on Sanibel have been generous with their time and their help in my research.

First of all, an inadequate thank-you for his unique, invaluable and long-term assistance, to Captain William E. Trefny of the Sanibel Police Department.

My thanks, also, to Carol Kranichfeld, Shirlene Grasgreen, George Campbell, Dee Slinkard, Jean Wood, Walter Klie and Christine Olsen.

And, off-island, to Dr. Richard J. Neudorfer and, once again, Dr. Martin Dolgin.

CHAPTER ONE

THE TWO MEN LOPED DOWN THE BEACH. WELL, ONE OF them loped: the tall one, with the long neck hanging slightly forward from hunched shoulders like a tortoise on long legs, a peaked canvas cap pulled over an inquisitive nose, knobby knees under baggy Bermuda shorts. The other—stocky, square, with short, powerful legs, a blunt-featured face, the alert, aggressive air of a terrier, younger by a dozen years or more— took a step and a half to every one of the Tortoise's, his feet rolling quickly from heel to toe as the double set of footprints followed them along the shore.

"I can't believe you're doing this to me," the Terrier yapped.

"To *you.* I'm doing it to *you.* If I went down in a plane it would be happening to *you.*"

"A whole year of sweat and agony!"

"*Your* sweat, right? Only yours."

They passed me as I stooped to the sand to pick up a small translucent shell. The sun baked the backs of my legs and the thin cotton of the worn blue shirt of Elliot's that I wore over an old pair of shorts. I wandered on down the beach behind the two

1

men, scrunching the sand with my bare toes. It was a seemingly endless beach, a strip of white sand stretching to the horizon, with a gray line running the entire length of it where the tide had deposited dead fish. Very still, very hot, all but deserted. What activity there was, was lethargic. A half-dozen human figures scattered in diminishing perspective down the long stretch of hard-packed sand at the water's edge peered downwards, looking for shells. A flock of gray-and-white gulls wheeled and flapped lazily above the greenish water of the Gulf of Mexico. The defunct fish, of course, simply lay there. As I moved down the beach in the wake of the two men, the flat, nasal voice of the Tortoise drifted back to me: "I said, go ahead! Leave me out of it, go ahead. You can have the material. Blood you're not going to get."

"Goddam it, you can't just walk away! You created this situation! You're responsible!"

"Depends where you're standing. P.O.V., like they say."

I wondered idly what enterprise had generated this heated argument. Business of some kind. Manufacturing. Import-export. Textiles. The vocal cadences were very much New York.

I stooped to pick up another shell, all ivory and pearly rose. A lovely languor suffused me. Sun, sand, water, warm tropical air. Paradise. I walked on, noting, to my right, two hundred yards across the sand, the various places of lodging running parallel to the shore, nestled unobtrusively between pepper trees and saw palmettos, their screened balconies looking out on the Gulf, if you were lucky, or on the balcony across the way, if you were not. Tamarind Gardens. Island Harbor. The Pines.

I'd walk roughly a mile, I decided, and turn back.

Up ahead the Terrier was still barking away. "The really aggravating thing—the thing that really corrodes my gut, is that this whole mess is *unnecessary*! The girl isn't that bad!"

"My doctor advised me to avoid potentially fatal stress and that girl is a coronary on legs."

"If we get Bob Dana—he can do *anything*, you *know* that, look what he did with that redhead from London—"

"Bullshit, Dana. He's a fireman. He's for when you're going up in flames. I don't start out on a hazardous project with combustible material."

Building trade? But where did a girl come into it? No, there was a whiff of something less prosaic. It was no earthbound form of commerce they were debating. Advertising, possibly.

The Terrier was docile now, appeasing. "Ideally, no. Ideally, I agree with you. But it's not as though we have options. We've been all over the map with this thing. We were *lucky* to get Grafman behind it. Okay, so we have to play by his rules, we—"

"Jeez, kid, you really do coin a phrase."

"Okay!" The younger man exploded, red-faced. "You want to walk, fine. You want to write off a year of your life, no sweat. You don't have to prove anything? Hooray for you. You've been there, you've done it, one more credit, what do you care?" His chest heaved with anger. "This is my first chance! Maybe my *last!*"

"One and a half percent." The Tortoise chuckled, a sound like a scratchy violin in a high register. "You want me to give him one and a half percent. This horse's ass from L.A. I don't love you that much, sweetheart, like they say on the Coast."

They stopped moving, suddenly, and stood looking at something up ahead. I moved inland a few feet and glanced up the beach. A figure was wading in the shallow water; long, creamy legs, lushly curved torso covered by a scant strip of white, sun glinting on short corn-yellow hair, a placid peach-colored face. Drape her in a towel, sit her on a nineteenth-century riverbank, and you had a latter-day Renoir. Was that what this was all about? An advertising campaign? *The towel that Renoir painted?*

The avid younger man, watching her as she leaned over to pick up a shell, implored, "Sherm, what's wrong with that? You don't think that's *exciting*?"

"Only to the male of the bovine species."

"Christ! That body, that face, that—!"

"She's a blonde." The implication was that this flaw was fatal.

"Come on, Sherm, there are black *wigs.*"

"Hair is not the problem. The problem, in the words of Pedro Calderón de la Barca, is that her *personality* is blonde."

"Pedro who?"

"Maybe it was Tolstoy. Or Jacqueline Susann."

Thoroughly intrigued by this bizarre dialogue, I was making a pretense of searching the immediate area for shells. The man began pacing to the edge of the water and back again, rubbing his forehead with one hand and muttering, "Down the drain. Just like that. Down the goddam drain." The blonde, meanwhile, made her serene way across the sand toward a horseshoe-shaped compound of new-looking balconied buildings. I winced at the sight of them, sitting there just off the beach, all blazing white stucco and glass doors with the name scrawled in large script like a pretentious "Continental" restaurant: THE GULLS. Where the older beach apartments hid modestly among their tangles of local flora, this one jutted aggressively onto the tranquil shore, as humble and appropriate as a branch of the World Trade Center rising out of Loch Lomond.

Sherm, the Tortoise, scratched the back of his neck and said, "I'm going back."

"Think about it! Will you *think* about it?"

Sherm didn't reply. He loped back the way we had come, the backs of his legs bright pink below the baggy Bermudas. The younger man looked after him for a moment, his face undecided between fury and anguish, then rolled off, heel-toe, in the same direction as the blonde.

She, I saw, was heading for a pair of deck chairs. In one of these lounged a man with a face that belonged behind a closely guarded poker hand. His expensively trimmed Vandyke of battleship gray matched the receding hair on his head and a mat of the same on a chest that was beginning the inevitable descent to his waistline. He was smoking a cigarillo and speaking, with the confidence of one who is seldom interrupted, to a younger man sitting on the sand with his back to the Gulf, dressed, not very sensibly, in crisply tailored gray slacks and a white shirt with the sleeves rolled to the elbow.

The blond woman reached the chairs, scattered her handful of shells into the older man's lap, laughing, and dropped into the empty chair over which a scarlet towel was flung. Vandyke looked at her, his eyes traveling possessively over the lush terrain between golden head and coral toenails, a wanderer come home to his personal land of milk and honey. He reached for the scarlet towel as she stretched one elegant leg in his direction, and began to dry it with lingering strokes while he went back to saying whatever he was saying to the young man.

When the Terrier reached this group he plunked himself down in a disconsolate heap, and I casually ambled by them to hear what I could hear.

The blond beauty was speaking, in a voice that bubbled with a sense of well-being. "Everybody knows royalty is the worst. Under those high-neck dresses they're *wild*. *I* think she was gone on him from the minute he boarded the ship. The haughty stuff was just to get the upper hand. Sex on the high seas . . ."—laughing—"the ship rolling . . ."

"I'm going to take you out in a boat," Vandyke, threatening.

"Oh, let's *do* that!" She sat up. "There's a marina that rents party boats. We could all get an idea of what it was like, seeing the place from out there—"

The man in the slacks said something I couldn't hear.

"You don't have to know how to swim," the Terrier said, "to go on a boat around the *island*."

The man in the slacks spoke again, inaudibly.

"They have life preservers on board," the blonde assured him. "Mitch, make him say yes."

"The man won't go on a boat," Vandyke's raspy reply. "I can't force him."

There were no shells in the sand where they sat. There were no empty chairs in which I could logically rest. I could hardly stand there doing nothing: shamelessness has its limits. I moved on, circling the group to return to the water's edge. The man in the gray slacks stood up and I glanced sideways and saw his face, with a mild jolt of recognition.

I knew that face from somewhere: a boyish face, bland and seamless, low forehead topped by curly brown hair. Where had I met it? Since my arrival on the island I'd had no contact with anyone but a worried old cabdriver and the sleek, fiftyish manager in the front office of the Sea Grape Inn. Someone from home, then. Was he one of those nameless men in the village real estate office? Had I interviewed him for the *Reporter;* one of the political aspirants who ran for Board of Education posts? He looked a little young for that. Had I met him at a party somewhere?

I walked on, avoiding the dead fish, probing my memory for a clue to where and how I'd previously seen the man in the gray slacks. When that proved stubbornly unfruitful, I devised a fanciful scenario to explain the connection between the two men I'd followed down the beach, and between them and the group at The Gulls. The scenario was complicated and, as it turned out, dead wrong. At that moment, though, it was a pleasant diversion, icing on the cake. Here I was, snatched, suddenly, from the icy grip of a northern winter, transported to this sunbaked barrier island, this little emerald set in the subtropical sea (*this other Eden, demi-paradise . . . this blessed plot*, this Sanibel) . . . without a serious problem to burden me. Why not amuse myself?

By the time I'd walked my mile and turned back, there was no longer anyone sitting outside the glaring excrescence called The Gulls, and nowhere between there and the Sea Grape Inn was there a sign of the Tortoise. End of incident.

It would be something to bring the invalid; a gift of local color to lessen the tedium of enforced idleness.

CHAPTER TWO

IT WAS ALMOST THREE WHEN I CLIMBED THE OUTSIDE
stairway to the second floor of Section 4D and opened the door
on a cool white-and-grass-green living room. My mother's
voice, which could, depending on the circumstances, evoke
either Elizabeth Barrett Browning or Elizabeth Cady Stanton,
on this occasion came in a carefully neutral nonplaintive tone
down the corridor from her bedroom at the back of the apartment.

"Maggie?"

"Yes." I went along to the bedroom where she lay flat on
her back, surrounded by books, with a contraption straddling
her composed of a tilting bed tray and a clamp, that allowed her
to read in that position. "You all right? Can I get you something?"

She removed her glasses and looked up at me with dark,
stubborn eyes. "Before you give me an argument, I've figured
out how to do it and all I need is some shampoo."

"For God's sake, you can barely get to the bathroom to pee,
how do you propose—"

"I'm not going to lie here with my hair looking like tortured fishtails.'' My mother's imagery was always vivid, if somewhat obscure in its relevance.

"Mother, you're supposed to rest. You're supposed to relax, so the ruptured intervertebral disc will stop pressing on the nerve or whatever.''

"You've been talking to Dr. Cole.''

"Certainly. I don't know what possessed you to take up aerobic dancing anyway.''

"Have you never heard of keeping fit?'' I looked at her. She lowered her eyes. "It's a slipped disc, that's what it amounts to. And I can't lie here like this. What if someone comes to see me?''

Ah-ha. "Are you expecting someone?''

"It's not impossible.'' In other words, she'd met someone, on the beach or in one of the shopping malls, someone who had helped her with a deck chair or reached up for a box of Shredded Wheat on a high shelf beyond her reach, and from this she was busily building romance. Give her a "Good morning'' to work with and in an hour she would have completed a rough outline for *Tristan und Isolde*. In most other respects she was reasonably sensible, even shrewd.

"Just get the shampoo, Maggie, don't argue.''

I argued for a while, pointing out that only twenty-four hours earlier I had abandoned my home, my job and my husband (not much disturbed by the abandonment, as he was temporarily on a business trip in Peru) and flown a thousand miles to care for her because she was immobilized.

"If you're well enough to go through the contortions of hair washing,'' I demanded, "what am I doing here? I thought I heard you say that whenever you moved, an intolerable pain shot down your left buttock and the back of your thigh, and you might as well be dead.''

"I'll bite on a stick. Don't bug me, Maggie.'' Along the way in later life she had collected odd bits of contemporary slang, which, dated or not, she scattered indiscriminately among sentiments that owed a good deal to the Victorians.

In the end I went for the shampoo. A little indulgence was called for. There was nothing I could do about the pain she was suffering, but if it would alleviate the boredom and indignity of being invalided, a little ingenuity might get her hair washed. I added shampoo to the grocery list and went back down the outside stairway and along the pebbled path that led to the parking lot. A lizard, escaping from parking lots and automobiles, scuttled across the path to hide among the sea grape bushes. I found the small yellow Ford and drove out to the road.

My mother, in her constant search for an environment congenial both in climate and cultural amenities, had decided she'd found it at last when she accompanied friends to this Gulf Coast island one winter. Not being aware of the hurricane warning sent out to the world by John MacDonald, she was seduced by the bougainvillea-and-red-tile-roofed charm of the Sea Grape Inn and plunked down a great portion of the savings she and my father had put by on his ophthalmology practice and her librarianship, on the purchase of a two-bedroom apartment. Two bedrooms, so that there would be room for Elliot and myself and the boys when we came down.

In two years neither Elliot nor the boys had been able to arrange a visit, and this was the first time I'd managed the trip. She, instead, had come north in the summer.

I'd been against the move, thinking of hurricanes. "It's a good investment," she'd insisted. "They rent it for you at stupendous rates when you're not using it yourself." It turned out, of course, that renters were interested in renting it during precisely those winter months for which she herself had purchased it. "There are writers and painters living here," she'd offered as an unanswerable argument, "chamber music concerts. It's culturally alive." She had yet to meet a writer or painter and the music had to be imported, infrequently, from Chicago and Cincinnati.

But she lived in hope. Also in sun and soft air, with hibiscus and papaya trees, with strange and colorful birds, with the great sweep of the Gulf and the occasional gallant in the supermarket. It was far from a hardship situation. I still worried about hurricanes, but then, I've always had a propensity for anticipating the wrong crisis.

Following her explicit instructions, I drove up to the main intersection and turned down Periwinkle Way, the long main street lined on both sides with tall, rather tatty-looking grayish-green casuarina trees. At the very end of Periwinkle was Bailey's, a magnificently comprehensive store supplying everything from lamps and shovels to cottage cheese and cooking wine. I bought vegetables, a chicken, the shampoo and also the large basin and plastic ground cloth the ingenious plan required.

Returning with my bulging shopping bag, I climbed the stairs to the second-floor landing and heard, from behind the outer, louvered door of the apartment next to my mother's, the unexpected sound of a Haydn symphony. That everlasting "Clock," of course. You'd think with a composer whose last opus numbered five thousand or thereabouts, they could find something to play that was a little less predictable.

"You had a phone call," my mother reported as I swept the radio dial back and forth searching for the Haydn.

"The boys?" I asked quickly. "Elliot?"

"No. It was C.B."

"*Greenfield?*" Charles Benjamin Greenfield. My employer. My confederate. My adversary. My ally. My indispensable affliction. Invariably my mother called him by his initials, making him sound like the man whose Biblical epics he had once described as Scriptural jelly beans. I switched off the radio, not having found Haydn.

What urgency had arisen that Greenfield had to reach me after a mere twenty-four-hour separation? Had there been a crisis at the *Reporter?* If so, what could I do about it at this distance? Had my house burned to the ground? If it had, the police would hardly have run to Greenfield with the news—they'd been told that the Olivers knew where I'd be, and had my key. *And* my dog.

"Ask for operator seven," my mother instructed.

While I waited for operator seven to make the connection, I envisaged the three-story white frame house on Poplar Avenue, with its shallow turn-of-the-century front porch, tall, narrow ground-floor windows, mansard roof, the first-floor rooms given over to the machinery and tiny staff of the *Sloan's Ford*

Reporter, the third floor to Greenfield's living quarters, and on the floor between, the one long room running front to back, with its wall of overflowing bookshelves, its senescent armchairs, its international litter of newspapers, periodicals, clippings, Greenfield sitting at his big cluttered oak desk, making illegible scribbles on scraps of paper, the phone, lost somewhere under the drift of papers, ringing. . . .

"Maggie." A statement, not a question. He had put in a call to Maggie, therefore Maggie it must be. The telephone company would not connect him with Indira Gandhi instead if they were interested in their own survival.

"Yes. What's wrong? I assume something is wrong."

Silence. Then, "How you can ask that," he said, "given the present state of the world, puts a severe strain on my comprehension."

"You know what I mean. Something *new*."

"The answer is yes." Significant pause. "My copy of the Schumann," portentously, "seems to be missing."

My God, missing sheet music! He's been sitting there quietly fuming over the fact that I had removed myself from his dominion, until finally he'd come up with an excuse for reaching out over the miles to reclaim my attention. Missing music!

"You probably left it at Gordon's," I said, suppressing a smile.

"Gordon says no. It's possible you picked it up last Friday and took it home with you, in which case it's sitting in your locked house."

"Why would I pick up your music? I never have before." I tried to remember the end of the session in Gordon Oliver's study, the violin on the straight-backed chair, Greenfield closing his cello case, myself folding up the music on the piano rack. I hadn't gone near Greenfield's music stand.

"You were distracted that night." He was making it up as he went along. "It's probably sitting in your living room. I need it. How am I going to get it?"

"Why do you need it?" A sudden small clutch of anxiety. Someone was going to replace me, usurp my place at those Friday-night trio sessions, after all these years.

"*Why* do I need my *music*?" There was a pause, meant to convey that the Southern sun had fried my brains. "What else would I use"—voice dry as driftwood—"for wrapping fish? Does anyone have a key to your place?"

"Shirley. She's watering my plants."

"You'd think Gordon would have mentioned it. I'll get the key from her."

"Why don't you just ask her to look for it. I've told the police she'll be going in occasionally, so they won't challenge her. On the other hand, if they saw *you* fiddling with the lock—" Greenfield's relations with the Sloan's Ford police came under the heading of Precarious Détente. There had been a couple of incidents—of a criminal nature—which Greenfield had seen fit not only to investigate but, unforgivably, to resolve. All by himself. With my help. My own reception at headquarters was always a bit frosty.

"How much longer are you going to be down at that beach?" Making it sound like a vacation.

"I really couldn't say," I retorted. "Ronnie and Bootsie are coming by on the yacht tomorrow and we may just pop over to Port-au-Prince, or maybe drop in at Solange's villa on Virgin Gorda, an inappropriate place for Solange, I admit—"

"The trouble," he said slowly, "with your parodies of third-rate literature, is that they're fourth-rate. In a few words—or less—how much longer will your mother need your assistance?"

"Charlie, I can hardly consult her gluteus maximus for an estimate."

A pause while Greenfield came to grips with reality. When I'd confronted him, two days earlier, with the indisputable claim of an ailing parent on her only daughter's time and presence, he'd leaned back in his whining swivel chair, stared for a while at the mess of papers covering his huge desk, and finally asked, "Couldn't you bring her up here?"

I'd explained that the problem was she couldn't move without howling, and he'd said nothing, but I could see him wondering if she could possibly be put under anaesthetic for the duration of the trip. It was not lack of compassion that prompted this response but a deeply entrenched inability to accept any disruption of his way of life. I was part of the accustomed course of his day, his sounding board, his sparring partner, his chief reporter, his errand woman. He was a man of fossilized habit, and even the retirement of a regularly consulted editorial writer on the *Times* could cause him to refuse food and sit around running his hand through his thin smoky hair until it stood on end, giving him the forlorn and slightly demented look of someone newly bereaved.

I pictured him now, sitting there in an old sweater with a thread loose somewhere, long of limb, long of face, long on the quietly benevolent manner spiked with the cutting remark, a man impressed by neither Fortune 500 nor computer technologists, skeptical of the wisdom of space cowboys, loathing the nuclear-game players, demanding nothing of life but universal dedication to justice, public health, peace and the arts, the proper use of language, a limitless supply of good music, and the permanent availability of anyone or anything he happened to need. Also smart enough to know a dead end when he reached it.

"If you haven't put a good solid board under her mattress," he said finally, "do so." And broke the connection.

I took the shampoo into the bedroom and showed it to the invalid. "I see you have neighbors who listen to real music. Next door, as I came up, they were playing Haydn."

"That's Nettie Ruskin's apartment."

"She has a stereo, then. It couldn't be the radio. I've fooled with that dial fourteen times and got nothing but garbage."

"The signal on that station is very weak. Occasionally, around five o'clock, it comes through."

"What does?"

"The classical music station. For an hour or so."

"Oh." Well, we all know the South is a depressed part of the country.

It didn't bother my mother nearly as much as it did me that her stereo was in for repairs. The truth was that she listened to serious music because she approved of it in principle, but enjoyed only what was written in three-quarter time. A waltz, whether by courtesy of Ravel or Casey's strawberry blonde, reached her; all else was a necessary cultural exercise. It was my father who'd had the ear.

"Nettie and Hal are in Europe," she said. "Spain, of all places. All those late meals and lost luggage. I told her they were foolish to go to Spain at their age."

"How old are they?"

"My age."

"Oh, I see. Ancient."

"You could hardly call it young."

"You once told me 'young' was a state of mind."

"I was younger then."

"And what's 'young' now that you're ancient?"

She thought about it. "It's someone who doesn't mind being photographed in profile."

There are definitions that quiver with accuracy.

"Your friends," I said, "may have gone to the wrong country, but they picked the right time to travel. No trouble renting out the apartment in the winter months."

"It's not rented. That's her son. He's a writer." She looked vindicated for a moment, but honesty compelled her to add, "Not a *serious* writer. I mean he's not another Joyce Carol Oates."

(I could imagine Greenfield's response to that: "One is quite enough.")

"He's done some things on Broadway, I think. And some television. Nettie carries clippings in her wallet, of course. Once she came running down to the pool and made me get out in the middle of my laps to read something from the Baltimore *Sun*."

I looked out the bedroom window, across a red-tile roof and down a spill of bougainvillea to the pool. There were, happily, no kids thrashing around. "I think, before I start the chicken, I'll take a swim."

Off the living room beyond sliding glass doors was a screened balcony: small round glass-topped table, two wrought-iron chairs, bridal fern in a hanging basket and a rack for drying clothes. I took my slightly damp swimsuit from the rack. Music from Nettie Ruskin's apartment—the Moonlight Sonata, good Lord!—filtered out to the Ruskins' balcony, a scant ten feet from my mother's drying rack. I glanced in that direction. Sprawled on a chintz-covered chaise, holding a glass of milk and still wearing the peaked cap and baggy Bermuda shorts, was, apparently, Nettie Ruskin's son. Sherm the Tortoise.

CHAPTER THREE

MORNING. I PUT THE PLASTIC GROUND CLOTH I'D bought at Bailey's on the floor by the bed, a dining room chair covered in more plastic on the ground cloth, a basin of warm water on the chair, and my mother flat on her back, sideways across the bed with her hair in the basin. Sloppy but effective. Changing the water in the basin after the shampoo was a bit precarious, but a towel around her head between rinses kept the mess to a minimum. The process was accompanied by an extension of a conversation begun at breakfast.

"Maybe," the invalid suggested, "He resembles an actor you've seen on the screen. Someone you *feel* you've met but actually haven't. You're getting soap in my ears."

"Sorry. No, he couldn't look like anyone else. It's not a common kind of face. Dammit, it's maddening not to be able to remember. It obliterates everything else. Like getting something caught between your teeth. Life goes on without you. War, peace, all you can think about is that sliver between the molars."

Beyond the windows in the hazy morning sunlight a passing bird gave a raucous cry and received a distant answer.

"Could it be someone you were once involved with?" she asked. "Romantically?" I smiled. "I mean long ago," she went on, "in high school, for instance."

"I believe he was an infant at the time."

"Some people look younger than they are. Think about it. You had a lot of boyfriends in those days, one after another. I remember at least six. You kept getting rid of them. You'd say this one was 'superficial,' that one had 'too big an ego.' We'd barely get used to the one who ate his meals in a trench coat, when he was gone, and there was another one who played a tuba."

"I remember them all, and none of them looked remotely like this man."

She accepted defeat, briefly. "And he was on the beach," she mused, "with Nettie Ruskin's son . . ."

"I didn't say they were together, just that there seemed to be a connection."

"Well, next time you see him it'll probably come to you in a flash."

"What next time?"

"You're bound to run into him—the island isn't that big and there are only so many places for people to go. Periwinkle for restaurants and shops. The bird sanctuary, the lighthouse and Captiva for sightseeing. And the beach. That's the whole bag. Unless people stay cooped up in their rooms, you can't help meeting them here and there. Or why don't you simply ask Nettie's son who he is?"

"That would be a little cheeky, don't you think, inasmuch as Nettie's son and I are not in the least acquainted. All right, you're done. Hold on to that towel and I'll slide you back."

With the help of some gadget that simultaneously heated and brushed, I dried her hair into something like the framework of soft curls that once had sprung there of its own accord. She gave up on the mysterious man and started on the family.

"I wish the boys would come down for a visit. I don't know why Alan had to go to Colorado to be a geologist, there are plenty of rocks in the East. I hope when it's Matt's turn to graduate he'll choose something he can only do in New York or Florida."

I tried to imagine my younger son wanting to do anything

that could only be done in Florida. Impossible. I put the gadget away and showed her a mirror. "Hm," she said.

The birds were at it again, squawking at each other as they swooped over the beach.

"Where is this bird sanctuary you keep talking about?" I asked. "I might go take a look at it, if you'll be all right for a while."

She said she would be fine and insisted I write down the directions for getting there. The entire island was about fourteen miles long and a mile or so wide, but she gave me directions so laden with details designed to prevent me from taking the wrong turn and becoming irretrievably lost, that a route from Helsinki to the Bosporus would have been meager by comparison. When I left I stopped at the first real estate office I came to and acquired a map.

According to the map, the Wildlife Refuge, a.k.a. the bird sanctuary, sat roughly halfway along a road that ran more or less straight as an arrow between the connected islands of Sanibel and Captiva. *Captiva.* The name was seductive, suggesting a mysterious tropical forest heavy with the gold of filtered sun and the scent of frangipani. I decided to take the road straight to Captiva to see what sort of place it was, then explore the sanctuary at leisure on my way back.

It was more humid than it had been the day before; the morning haze hadn't cleared and the sky was bright but colorless. The Sanibel–Captiva road ran between massed wild shrubs and Brazilian pepper trees, a bicycle path snaking along beside the roadway. I passed two boys in cut-off jeans and sneakers pedaling along, their backs brown with sun, little orange flags flying from their bicycles. Farther on, a young couple were jogging, their faces blank and sweaty.

Eventually I found myself crossing a small cement bridge. The jungle of trees and bushes on either side of the road had thinned and the island had narrowed to a stretch of sand to the left of the bridge, dotted with pitted boulders. All the rest was water. I pulled off the road onto the edge of the beach, parked next to a station wagon and consulted the map. This, apparently, was something called Blind Pass and everything beyond it would be Captiva. I stepped out of the car and stretched, took off my sandals and walked about examining the gray pitted boulders: Some sort of coral they must be. On the far side of the bridge three middle-aged women waded cautiously, searching for shells. On the beach a small boy, waving the shell he held in his hand, ran along the shore toward a man farther up the beach, calling out triumphantly, "Look! Look—a king's ransom!"

Shelling was obviously an obsession on the island, the young, the old, the in-between, all roaming the sands, heads bent eagerly to the ground, forever straining their eyes. Even my mother, on a shelf in her living room, proudly displayed limpets, sundials, whelks, olives, miters, marginellas, arks, and a few dozen I hadn't bothered to look up in the large book on the shelf below that pictured and described a thousand varieties, some poisonous, that one could hope to find someday if one's legs and eyes held out. King's ransom was a conch, and conches, if I remembered correctly, could be deadly if the animal inside was still alive. With a small twinge of anxiety I watched the little boy. Would he suddenly drop the shell with an agonized cry, or keel over in a dead faint? He merely handed the shell to the man and danced around him in excitement.

I went back to the car, pulled out onto the road and proceeded into the heart of darkest Captiva. It was not exactly a dense tropical forest, but the road *was* narrow here, and winding, and trees and tangled bushes crowded the road on either side. Here and there I caught a glimpse of a bungalow hidden away among a cat's cradle of vines, branches and foliage, and occasionally, on the left, the road skirted the shore where Australian pines, bent by the winds, leaned out over the Gulf at a drunken angle.

This, I felt, was the island as the elements had fashioned it, the raw, untamed bar of sand, silt and plant life that tides and time and seaborne organisms had built up over the centuries. This was the way it had been long ago when—when what? I resolved to read a little history. In the meantime I rejoiced. No sign here that the World Trade Center was slowly encroaching.

And the next thing I saw, nailed to a tree, was a placard printed in bold black letters with the name of a firm of real estate agents.

The tree to which the notice was nailed was unlike any I'd ever seen. Tall as a three-story house, with feathery light-green foliage and a thick trunk from which the rough reddish bark was peeling, disclosing the pink, seal-smooth, naked-looking trunk beneath, it looked like a very large, painfully sunburned tourist. A few yards beyond the tree a track ran through the welter of scrub and branches, just wide enough for one car, and visible through a jumble of leaves, palm fronds and pine boughs, was the roof of a bungalow. On impulse I turned into the track and bumped along in the direction of the Gulf, wondering how I would ever back out of there.

A hundred yards or so down the track the wilderness, broken on one side only by a rough path that headed obliquely toward the water, gave way on the other side to a clearing of stubbly grass dotted with odd-looking trees and bisected by a walk made of wooden planks leading to the bungalow.

It was a square, low beach house of weathered wood siding with a peaked roof, a brick chimney and an entrance that consisted of three worn steps mounting to a screened porch. A bicycle leaned against the house; there was no sign of a car. As I took the key from the ignition a figure came scrambling around the side of the house, alert for trouble.

She looked to be in her late twenties, coltish, all arms and legs in earth-soiled jeans and a sleeveless cotton top, huge eyes, sharp little nose, hair the color of cork, rough-cut, sticking out around her face in several directions and falling into her eyes. In one grimy hand she held a trowel, in the other a plant with leathery leaves and a bulb like an onion at the bottom. She stopped about ten feet from the car, pointing her nose at me. I could almost see it twitching, like an animal sniffing a strange scent: friend or foe?

"Hi!" I got out of the car and walked around to where she stood. "I know I'm trespassing and I apologize, I just wanted some information."

"About the property?" She flung one arm accusingly toward the jungle on the far side of the track. "You can't buy it. *Nobody's* going to buy it. I'm going to stop it all. We've had enough!" The eyes flashed, the first time I'd seen gray eyes flash.

"Well, no, I—" But now I was curious. She was clearly referring to the sign on that naked tree. "Is there some question as to who owns that land?"

"That's entirely beside the point. Beside the point. Legal right is meaningless. There are laws that take precedence.

There's a moral issue here. Just forget about it. Forget about it.'' She waved dismissal with the hand holding the spade and turned back toward the house.

"I didn't come about the property," I said, and she stopped and looked back over her shoulder. "I was just curious about that strange tree with the notice nailed to it. What's it called?"

The sharpness left her small, pointed face, and a slow smile spread winningly across it. "You mean the gumbo-limbo?"

"Gumbo-limbo?" It sounded like a Caribbean dance or a can of soup.

"That's the African name for it. The botanical terminology is *Bursera simaruba*. They use the sap to make glue and varnish. I make tea from the leaves. It's very good, you can hardly smell the varnish. Would you like some?"

I wasn't certain my spirit of adventure extended to drinking varnish, and I was about to decline gracefully, but she was already heading for the back of the house.

"Just let me take care of the spider lily first." She gestured with the plant that dangled from her hand. "I'm separating the bulbs and spreading them around. They'll grow anywhere. *Hymenocallis latifolia*. Marvelous. My name is Sarah McChesney."

"Uh—Maggie Rome." I followed her around the side of the house to what anywhere else would have been a backyard. Here it looked like a nonconformist's botanical garden. Subtropical plants, trees and bushes grew in exotic profusion over the large plot of ground, an exuberant display.

"You're a visitor?" she asked, squatting and turning the earth carefully with the spade.

"My first visit. I have a mother who lives at the Sea Grape."

"The Sea Grape. Well, that's been here a while." She seemed to find the Sea Grape innocent of wrongdoing. "That's the problem, you see, it's not morally defensible to prevent new people from coming here to enjoy the island, that's obvious. On the other hand, where will it stop? How much more building can we *allow*? It's *already* gone too far. This is a *small island*. Ecologically it can't *sustain* a large population. The aquifers under the island are *limited*. That's what they refuse to recognize. Natural resources are limited! They have a *limit*! Every time those dredging machines bite into the— These commercial shelling companies, you know? The *damage* they've done! Digging up the entire seabed! The dredging has put holes in the claypan—'' Her voice quivered, the gray eyes blazed up at me, passionately concerned. "Do you know, the *water table* is already dangerously *low*?"

She got up, went to where a hose was attached to an outside faucet, and turned it on. "When my parents bought this house there wasn't even a causeway to the island, people had to get here by ferry. There weren't any shopping centers or *boutiques.*" Her lips curled around the word with infinite contempt as she began to water the hole she'd dug. "But of course the *business* interests decided that what the birds and fish and mangroves needed was a little high-density *construction.* There's a war going on, you know. We've got a rate-of-growth ordinance, but the developers are fighting for permits, some of the locals are fighting some of the natives, some are fighting the developers.'' She planted the bulb in the wet hole, took a handful of something from a sack, sprinkled it around and closed the hole with the earth she'd dug up, patting it down carefully. "The city council is fighting, and the planning board—we're all fighting. And I'm damned—I really am *damned*—if that high-priced call girl is going to build herself a big fat resort house next door to *me*!" She stood up and wiped her hands on her jeans.

"Someone's already made a bid for it?"

"She can just take her little fat-cat face and her middle-aged lover with his big plans and his quarter-million dollars, and go to Miami or Pompano with all the other high-rise types!" She shook hair out of her eyes. "Okay! Let's have tea."

"Mm—no, thanks, I have to get back. This is a wonderful garden. I wish I knew what I was looking at."

Immediately she introduced me. Nicker bean and inkberry, wax myrtle, joewood, a wild lime tree, tamarind and bay cedar . . . we circled the yard and at the back I noticed the beginning of another wooden plank walk.

"Where does this go?"

"We have some beachfront." I followed her through an opening in a group of coco plum bushes, down the wood planks between clumps of tall wild grass, and there before us was the long sweep of white sand and the pale-green expanse of the Gulf.

I smiled, looking out at the water. "You can hardly blame people for wanting to share this."

"Yes, and if they keep building, there'll be nothing here to share."

I nodded and idly reached to pluck a long strand of the bleached grass.

"Don't!" Her hand flew up, palm out, to stop me. "You mustn't pick those, they're sea oats, they keep the beach from eroding." There followed a description of the network of rhizomes under the sand and the rooting at the nodes of stems.

"Are you a botanist?"

"I have a degree. I work for the Conservation Foundation." She had wandered out to the tidemark and suddenly stooped and picked up what looked like an unattractive necklace strung with tiny papery envelopes. "Sand collar," she said. Holding it carefully, she wandered about until she found a small rock and went back to the water. "Full of eggs. They'll hatch in the water." She put the sand collar under the water and the rock on top.

From the direction of the track in front of the house there was the sound of a car horn; two peremptory beeps. Sarah's head whipped around. She stood for a moment, poised for flight like a doe who's heard a rifle shot, then she darted, not away, but up the wood planks toward the intruder.

Going after her through the gap in the coco plums and across the yard, I realized my car was blocking the track. I couldn't imagine the track led anywhere habitable beyond this point, but perhaps farther down there was access to "the property." I rounded the side of the house and saw Sarah approaching a pale-blue Dodge drawn up behind the Ford. A woman stepped out of the car. She was wearing white slacks and a thin flowered shirt, but even with clothes on there was no mistaking the blond Renoir from the beach. Against the vigorous, wild growth of the uncleared land behind her, she looked like a long-stemmed rose in a florist's box; flawless but out of place. She didn't seem to know it; flushed with the heady wine of hope, youth, health, beauty, and the promise of excitement, she was glorying in herself.

"Hi!" She smiled—a dazzling smile. "We're going down to look at the beach. I just love Captiva. You are so *lucky* to have a place of your own here. I'm keeping my fingers crossed about getting this property. If we do, I don't think I'll ever want to leave."

Sarah was wearing her charming smile. "Would you mind backing out to the road, please, so my friend can get out?"

"Sure thing." She turned and spoke to the man in the passenger seat, who slid behind the wheel and began to reverse the car. To Sarah she said, "That's why I tooted the horn. I thought, Oh Lord, what if she has company that wants to leave while we're down on the beach." She smiled again, instant radiance.

"That was very thoughtful." Sarah came back to where I was standing. "Miss Fat Cat," she murmured. "But the man with her isn't the one who's paying the bills. She has a wandering eye, that one."

"You were very polite to her." I didn't bother to hide my surprise.

"Always be nice to the enemy," she said. "It keeps them off guard."

I could feel my eyebrows go up, but I thanked her for showing me around, crossed to my car and backed carefully down the rutted track. The pale-blue Dodge stood on the verge of the road waiting for me to get out of the way. I caught a glimpse of the man behind the wheel—youngish, casual, dark-haired, T-shirted, flaunting virility. A far cry from the man on the beach with the Vandyke of battleship gray. Maybe that was the idea.

Driving on toward the northern tip of Captiva, I thought about the oddly assorted group on the beach. The blonde, apparently, was not a model for a towel commercial. Following my mother's revelation the day before about Nettie Ruskin's son, the more likely explanation was that she was an actress (of whom Ruskin disapproved) and that some sort of theatrical production was in progress. Ruskin, I supposed, was involved as a writer, but what the rest of the men were up to and what the whole crew was doing on this island I couldn't imagine. Had the Vandyke and the blonde come down here to look for property and been followed by the others? But why would they follow? Had Ruskin come down to occupy his parents' empty apartment and brought the others with him? But why would they come, and why were none of them—as far as I could tell—sharing the apartment? And why did I care? Well, they were a curious lot, and I had nothing else at the moment at which to point my inquisitive reporter's nose.

In any case, I thought, the blonde would not have an easy time of it as a prospective neighbor of that clever colt, that wary doe, that fiercely committed and surprisingly wily creature, Sarah McChesney.

Getting fanciful, Maggie, I told myself. Terriers, tortoises, colts. A bloody menagerie I had collected.

I stopped at a General Store, which, together with a post office and a firehouse, seemed to constitute the only commercial center on Captiva, bought myself a container of milk, some cheese and a banana, found a bit of public beach and sat on the sand nibbling and sipping and watching the water shade from pale jade at the shore to brownish green farther out and finally to deep dark green with a line of white foam. A familiar string of dead fish garnished the beach. Three or four people wandered along the water's edge, singly, shelling. Time and tranquillity seemed to be bottomless commodities here. They weren't, of course. There was ferment everywhere—red tide in the water killing the fish, sand everlastingly being pulled away from the sea oats, birds getting drunk on the pepper-tree berries, developers bulldozing the trees, the Conservation Foundation fighting the developers, Ruskin and the Terrier engaged in a heated tug-of-war. . . .

CHAPTER FOUR

BY THE TIME I WOUND MY WAY BACK DOWN THE length of Captiva, over the small bridge at Blind Pass and onto the Sanibel portion of the Sanibel–Captiva road, I realized it would be too late to give the bird sanctuary the time it deserved and still get back at a reasonable hour. I'd left lunch for my mother—sliced turkey sandwich and a thermos of tea—but human company could not be stored and unwrapped for use when needed. Regretfully, I postponed the sanctuary trip and gave myself instead the treat of stopping at the MacIntosh bookstore on Periwinkle Way to pick up a book on the history of the islands.

The bookstore occupied what seemed once to have been someone's white frame house. With its long narrow porch across the front, it reminded me somewhat of Greenfield's combined offices and living quarters, though Greenfield's house was taller, with a New England austerity about it, and was probably, at the moment, covered in snow. The MacIntosh bookstore had a more leisurely look, with just a hint of the ramshackle in the porch laden with tables of sale books, and it stood in the shade of a Hong Kong orchid tree dripping with vermilion blossoms.

I walked in and saw, among the people wandering about scanning the shelves, the man with the crisp gray slacks and white shirt whose boyish, low-browed face had been nagging at my memory. My mother was one of those people who are invariably accurate in their predictions concerning trivial matters.

Gray Slacks was taking a book from one of the shelves in a section marked "Sanibel Flora and Fauna," and my impulse was to put an end to frustration by simply accosting him. Simple enough in theory, impossible in practice. "Haven't we met before?" is a woman wearing sandwich boards saying *Man Wanted*. An innocent comment on the interesting flora of the island unfortunately depends, for its segue to the flora of his native state, on the man's willingness to converse. And in any case it's only sandwich boards Scarsdale style.

Why not, I decided, let *him* take the initiative? If his face was familiar to me, he might very well recognize *mine* and say something. I moved over to the bookshelves next to where he stood. When he looked up from flipping through the book he'd taken from the shelf, I'd be in his line of vision, he'd recognize me, say, "Oh! Hello. I'm so-and-so. We met at—" and I could go back to worrying about foreign policy. I picked a book at random from a nearby shelf. By chance, a history of the islands. I opened it. Drawings of Indians, Spanish galleons, pirates . . . real pirates? Apparently. Jesuit missionaries, colonists, maps, place-names—Punta Rassa, Point Ybel, Caloosa Hatchee . . . When I looked up from the book the gray slacks were gone. I glanced around and saw his back disappearing through the door, a wrapped book under his arm. Uncivilized lout. He might have said *something*.

I took the history of the islands to the man at the desk, paid for it, and drove home to the Sea Grape. There was no music from the Ruskin apartment when I climbed the outside stairway. Not a note, not even "Clair de Lune." I wondered if perhaps "Nettie's son" 's fight with the Terrier had put an end to his reason for being here and he'd packed up and gone. But no. When I descended again at dusk for a pre-dinner swim, there he was, cleaving the waters of the pool.

He swam with all the buoyant ease of a rock, his progress across the length of the pool marked by a series of geyser-like eruptions, one each time an arm hit the water. His legs, as far as I could see, simply trailed behind.

I put my towel and robe on a plastic chair, and returned the affable smile of a white-haired man who was stretched out alongside his wife just as they'd been when I'd come down to swim the day before. He had a nose that turned up, she a mouth that turned down. Actually he'd been sitting up when I'd first seen them, and she'd said, "Lie flat, you'll get wrinkles in your tan." He, by God, had obeyed. Now she looked up at the deepening slate-blue of the sky, announced that it was time to go in, and picked up a beach bag shaped and painted to resemble a whale.

With their departure the pool area was deserted except for Ruskin and myself. I swam in the heavy wash of his thrashing until, to my great relief, he stopped at the shallow end and lounged against the tiles breathing deeply, occasionally kicking feebly with his legs. I did a satisfying number of laps while he soaked there, and by the time he climbed out I, too, felt ready to quit the pool. I swam one more length for good measure, and as I reached the far end a pair of Nike running shoes appeared on the tile above my eyes. It was the Terrier. He looked a little drained, as though perpetual motion was beginning to wear him down, but he proceeded jauntily enough to where Ruskin was taking his towel from a chair next to those abandoned by the people with unwrinkled tans.

I left the pool in time to hear their opening exchange.

"It's nice," the younger man said, "you have time for swimming and all kinds of leisure activities. I'm glad for you, Sherm."

Ruskin dabbed at his dripping face. "I thought they had a pool at The Gulls. What'd they do, turn it into a disco? Take off your shoes, jump in, be my guest."

"No time for it, I've got work to do."

"Yah? How's it going?"

"Good. Very good."

"Wonder boy perform any miracles yet? Find a new ending? Rewrite the first act?"

"He's getting there."

"Isn't that great. And what does he say about the number one problem?"

"Thea? He doesn't say it's a problem."

"No? What does he say about the character?"

"Nothing, so far."

"He doesn't say a hell of a lot, does he."

"Well, actually, no. He's got laryngitis."

"Laryngitis. How about that. What do you use to communicate, a slate?"

"We manage. He's not jumping in with both feet, Sherm. I wouldn't trust one of those guys who come up with easy answers. He's careful, won't commit himself without giving something a lot of thought. Grafman asked him yesterday to come up with an alternative approach to that scene where Thea talks to the girls—just to see how—you know—how he's thinking. He just shook his head, very calm, and wrote down 'Don't rush, we'll get there.' "

"He wrote that down? Well, that's good, shows he knows how to work a pen."

"He knows what he's doing, Sherm. He definitely gives me that impression. Confident. He has a calm, confident smile and he smiles a lot. And he's got good credits."

"Good *sitcom* credits, Webber." Ruskin said it gently, as though explaining to a child.

"No, listen, he comes from a musical background, Grafman told me. He once studied oboe."

"That's going to help a lot." Ruskin began to towel his graying black hair vigorously. "So everything's fine. Is that what you dropped by to tell me?"

"Well, actually, there—um—seems to be another hitch."

Ruskin peered out suspiciously from between the folds of the towel. I dried my toes. Very slowly.

"The thing is," Webber the Terrier went on, "he wants your name off the script." There was an ominous silence from the towel. Webber looked away and his voice rose. "I know, I know, he's got balls—"

Ruskin whipped the towel from his head and roared, "Not for long!"

"Grafman told him it was asking a lot. *I* told him there was no way we could ask you—"

"But you're asking, aren't you! That's what you're doing here. You're seriously asking me—"

Webber abandoned any pretense at a cool, businesslike posture. His face grew red and sweaty and he began to heel-toe back and forth between the chair and the edge of the pool. "He's adamant, Sherm! This guy acts like he's got six shows lined up waiting for his signature and he doesn't need—"

"He's got nothing! He's one more hack on the assembly line out there! He'd sell his wife and kids and all his girlfriends for a chance at this!"

"Sherm, I was *there*! He *means* it! He says if he doesn't get sole credit he's not interested! And he *means* it! Sherm, I gave up half a percent so you'd only have to give him *one*. If we lose him—for Christ's sake, there's a *time* limit! Grafman isn't going to be involved with this forever, he's got other projects, he'll *drop* this if Persky leaves! We could lose the whole ballg—"

"Lose! What am *I* going to lose? You already conned me out of half my points! How much am I supposed to give up to save your brilliant future? I've been mugged by experts, kid, but I never lost half as much to a druggie with a knife as you got out of me with a couple of sobs! Listen, let me tell you something, this Persky is either certifiably nuts or he's a graduate of the L.A. school of moral turpitude. He's got my hundred and twenty pages in his hands, he hasn't come up with word one, and he wants *my* name off the script? Who's his agent, Machiavelli?"

"He hasn't talked to his agent. Because of the laryngitis. He writes notes to Grafman, Grafman calls the agent, the agent says, well, Alvin has assessed the situation and this is what he wants."

Ruskin pulled a terrycloth shirt over his head. "Webber, here's what you do. You tell Grafman to call Mr. Ruskin's agent. Mr. Ruskin's agent will tell him that Mr. Ruskin has assessed Mr. Persky's assessment, and that any decision as to whether or not Mr. Ruskin's name will *remain* on that script will be made by Mr. *Ruskin, after* he sees to what extent Mr. *Persky* has crapped it up!" Ruskin draped the towel over his hunched shoulders and loped off across the grass.

Webber shouted after him, "You want one percent of *noth-*

ing? Because that's what you'll have! Nothing!'' A quietly dressed couple, on their way to dinner somewhere, emerged from the 4B house and regarded him with slightly pained expressions as he sprinted after Ruskin. ''Wait! Wait, you bastard!''

The female half of the couple caught my eye as I started up the path. I shook my head, hypocrite that I am, planting myself firmly on the side of restrained behavior, and continued up the path and up the stairs where a lot of muted but urgent sound was going on behind the Ruskins' door. It continued until, getting into dry clothes, I heard the slam of the same door. Who, I wondered, was the demanding Mr. Persky? The role of Grafman seemed to fit what I'd seen of the Vandyke, and ''Thea,'' presumably, was the blonde. The only other apparent participant was the man in the gray slacks and he couldn't be Mr. Persky because I'd never met a Mr. Persky.

As I put my suit out to dry on the balcony rack I noticed the hanging plant was yellowing. The phone rang in the Ruskin apartment and I heard ''Sherm'' Ruskin's nasal voice yet again. Tense now, and weary. ''—he wants to *buy* a loft? Why can't he *rent* one, like an ordinary poor person? . . . Well, who the hell's going to pay for it? . . . I don't need another investment.'' He appeared on his balcony wrapped in a towel, telephone receiver tucked under the ear, dripping swim trunks in his hands. I plucked yellowed leaves from the plant.

''A whole loft to develop some pictures! Private space! He's twenty goddam years old. When I was twenty the only private space I had was my parents' bathroom.'' He spread his swim trunks on a wicker table. I picked up the plant mister and sprayed.

''Roz, I can't deal with this now, things are not going well down here. The matter is I'm being buried alive. I *can't* turn my back, I put a *year* into it. . . . I don't know when I'll be home. . . . Because there's still a chance. Maybe.'' He went back into his living room. ''Just an idea I have.'' His voice dwindled.

I stayed on the balcony watching the darkness creep over a Spanish bayonet at the corner of a pebbled path. Poor Ruskin. His voice was heavy with the impotence of someone being blackmailed. Pay up, or take the consequences. Damned if he paid, damned if he didn't.

I went in to take the fish from its marinade and put it in the oven. I wondered what sort of man this Mr. Persky was, with his implacable ultimata: Give me this, give me that or I bring the whole thing crashing to the ground, I leave you stranded, pack my bags and get on the next—

I almost dropped the fish.

"The airport!" I shrieked.

It was a foolish thing to do; my mother, in her bedroom, sat up abruptly and let out a howl. I rushed to help her, remorseful but euphoric. I'd remembered where I'd seen the man in the gray slacks.

"He was at the airport in Fort Myers," I told her when she'd calmed down. "At the baggage claim. Standing at the next carousel. I noticed him because he was the only person left from some previous flight. There were three suitcases going around, and he couldn't find his. I thought they'd sent the poor man's bag to Hawaii, but when the third bag came around, that was it, and he went off. *That's* who it is! Thank God! Well, no wonder he didn't know me."

"Every time I take a trip," my mother said weakly, "I notice how everyone's suitcase looks exactly like everyone else's."

I didn't quite follow that observation, but ignored it, giddy with relief. "Let's break open that bottle of Riesling in the refrigerator and have it with dinner!"

CHAPTER FIVE

I WOKE TO A HUMID MORNING, A FEW RAGS OF SOILED-looking clouds drifting across a sky of bluebird-blue. A sponge bath for the patient, a shower for me. Breakfast. The news, on television, none of it good for anyone but a professional war-wager, frigid temperatures up north. My mother watched the weather report avidly. The daily weather report in Chicago, New York and Boston is a major source of satisfaction for Northerners temporarily residing in the State of Florida. I took the used towels, odds and ends, down to the laundry room and returned with them washed and dried. Straightened the beds. It was a little after ten when there was a knock at the door. Could this finally be my mother's gallant supermarket acquaintance?

It was the radiant blonde: Thea, if my assumptions were correct. Glowing, in tomato-red shorts and a silky white shirt. For one disoriented moment I wondered why she'd come to see me.

"Um—Sherman Ruskin? Do I have the wrong apartment?"

"Next door," I pointed.

"Sorry to bother you." Brilliant smile, Gulf-green eyes not quite looking at you, preoccupied with the private rapture of being who she was. She turned away and I shut the door and

33

pondered the unlikeliness of this visit. Had she been sent to persuade Ruskin to bow to the inevitable? Strange tactics, considering his immunity to her charms. I took two postcards and a pen out to the table on the balcony, not without the ignoble thought that I might hear something, but Ruskin was playing music again. Excerpts from *Carmen*, wouldn't you know, and it scrambled whatever conversation there was. I sent sandpipers on the beach to Alan, gulls beyond a palm tree to Matt.

A visitor did arrive, just before noon, but not one likely to trigger any romantic fantasies. She was a diminutive, doll-like woman in her late sixties, with faded blue eyes and thinning reddish hair, who asked chirpingly after my mother and made her way back to the bedroom for a chat. I persuaded her to stay for lunch, prepared a tuna salad and iced tea, set it on a tray—plates, glasses, the works—and took my leave. The bird sanctuary today, and no detours, except for a quick lunch. Eating out was one of my favorite pastimes and I'd noticed a mall on Periwinkle Way full of attractive-looking shops. Bound to be something appetizing in that area.

The whole length of Periwinkle, a few feet in from the road and parallel to it, a bicycle path ran straight as a telephone wire, except that around each of the hundred-odd casuarinas lining the road, it made a small semicircle. Up ahead I could see the wavering orange flags of half a dozen bicycles going blithely along, swooping around a tree, then carrying on until the next one, as they headed for the shopping centers. One of the bicycles, however, was wobbling precariously from side to side, barely making it around the casuarinas, and as I passed it I realized it was Ruskin's peaked cap I was looking at and his knobby kness pumping away. His natural aptitudes, I decided, must be confined to his work: he had none at all for his leisure-time pursuits.

I pulled into the parking lot, left the car, walked through the pleasant courtyard of trees and grass around which the glossy shops were clustered, and up to the wooden walkway that led past all the goodies. Beachware, kitchenware, local crafts. Souvenirs and gourmet delicacies. All the usual, done up with ribbons. From Cape Cod to Carmel—probably from Nairobi to Nome—in these watering places only the labels change. I came suddenly to a plate-glass front that displayed nothing but people at work. *The Island Reporter.* A newspaper office, by God.

With that deceptive feeling of comradeship one gets when encountering a fellow countryman in foreign parts, I all but marched in to announce that I, too, worked on a smalltown paper. I looked it over. There wasn't much physical resemblance between this businesslike interior and Greenfield's ground-floor rooms with their scuffed linoleum floors and secondhand tables strewn with pages of copy, jam jars of pencils, Calli's battery of scissors, Stewart's scribbled first drafts of leads, Helen's gingersnaps and staplers. Here, in the front office, sat a number of proper desks, each with its IBM Selectric and busy telephone, stacks of important-looking papers, efficient-looking staff, large, orderly bulletin board. A major-league look about the whole place.

I was about to turn away when a coltish figure came scurrying forward down the corridor from a back room. Sarah McChesney, scrubbed and wearing a red T-shirt and clean jeans, with a Polaroid suspended from a strap around her neck, but otherwise unchanged, her hair looking as though it had been combed by a gale. She came straight at me and I stepped aside just in time to avoid being hit by the door as she erupted.

She saw me, glared, flashed a brief, beguiling smile, and returned to the glare. "What good is it, contributing to the paper, writing articles on ecological responsibility, pointing out the island's vulnerability, takes me days to write them, days, and who reads them, who cares? The tourists come for their two weeks, use up our resources and go home and never think about us again. Do they ever go to a meeting of the planning commission? Do they take an interest? Nobody cares. The whole world is venal." With a mild shock, I realized there were tears glistening in her eyes. "I can talk myself hoarse at a public hearing, as long as nobody's violating the comprehensive land-use regulations, who's interested in preserving that tract of land? Ninety percent of the island is in the real estate business! It's tragic, absolutely tragic! Look at that!" She tilted her chin to indicate something going on in the courtyard.

Beside an ornamental pool in which a slender fountain spurted delicately from a metal sculpture, Thea was being photographed, apparently for public consumption. With one hand on a metal reproduction of a heron, she bestowed her glorious smile on the camera held by a young woman who shifted her position expertly from below to on high and from side to side as she aimed at her subject from different angles. Despite the smile, Thea looked a little paler than she had a few hours before, as though she'd powdered her face.

"Fat Cat will be all over the paper," Sarah said moodily, "and the tourists will lap it up. She's got her entourage over there on the benches. Always eating. Now it's ice cream."

I followed her glance, saw a restaurant on the far side of the courtyard, some benches on the adjacent walkway, people on the benches.

"They were all at *the property* an hour ago. On the beach. Having a *picnic*. Food all around, paper cups, soda bottles, *garbage*. I called Liddell, the realtor, but nobody answered. They're always out selling, selling, selling. *Garbage* on the *beach*! And the property isn't *his* yet. It's got to stop. They were all there, the man who pays the bills, the other two. Now she's going to pick up Leroy again. A male harem, she has."

"Leroy?"

"You saw him yesterday. In the car with her."

Ah, Mr. Virility. "So you know him."

"He works at the marina. While she was having her *picnic* with the others, she announced she was going to the Refuge this afternoon to look at the birds. Birds! Can you see her interested in birds? It's Leroy, you can bet on it." She tapped the camera at her side with long, graceful, stained fingers and pursed her mouth with a resolute air. "If one picture is worth a thousand words, it's certainly worth two acres. Would a man who pays the bills buy property for a woman after he's seen proof that she's carrying on behind his back? No, he would not. He certainly would not."

I was shocked. Sarah McChesney, so morally fastidious, planning to point a camera at two people in an intimate embrace? Even in the interests of ecological preservation?

"Of course," I said carefully, "I know nothing about this particular property, but it seems logical that if the real estate people don't sell to one person, they'll go right on to the next one who meets the price. You can't hope to—um—undermine every deal that comes along."

"I have to buy *time*," she retorted, as though I were being obtuse. "I need *time*. If we get that private funding, we'll be in a position to buy the property. Do you realize what that would mean for the island eco system, not to mention the native plant nursery?" She shook hair out of her eyes. "I have to be ruthless." A brusque wave of the hand and she darted off to the parking lot, where her bicycle was chained to a post. I watched her ride off, as smoothly as though she were sailing. Ruthless Sarah. I couldn't imagine her actually going through with it.

I saw Thea had finished her posing at the fountain and was heading for the benches around the restaurant across the courtyard.

The restaurant looked attractive. It proved to be popular as well. The benches on the walkway were filled with people apparently waiting for tables. Over a PA system a disembodied voice called out "Dewar, party of three!" and an already well-fed trio rose from a bench and hastened inside. I looked around for a restaurant without a waiting line, but saw nothing that looked as though it had ever heard of a salad, and made my way past the bench to one side of the restaurant entrance where Thea had joined Webber, the man from the airport, still wearing the gray slacks, and Grafman—if that was his name—all of them having a postpicnic dessert of ice cream cones. The young man in the restaurant who seemed to be in charge of the public announcements told me I could wait outside. I obeyed, stood with my face in the sun. On the bench next to me Webber was leaning forward intently, his terrier face apprehensive.

"What if I bring it down a half-tone?" he was saying, while his cone dripped, disregarded, "and change the release, broaden it, you know—quarter notes there instead of eighths—"

Thea looked mildly unhappy. She regarded her strawberry ice cream without enthusiasm and said, "That's not the problem, Gary. It's just wrong for me. The whole song is too— too—"

"Strident," put in Grafman, licking away contentedly. "Too coarse. We need something more lyrical."

"*Everything's* lyrical! The song with the girls is lyrical. The boat song is lyrical. This one is supposed to be *fiery*. You loved it when you first heard it!"

Grafman shrugged. "It wasn't Thea singing it."

"What do *you* think, Alvin?" Webber turned to the man from the airport, who sat by impassively biting small chunks from his cone. "You like the song? You think we should dump it? Or what?"

"Alvin," with a neutral, detached expression, made a few hoarse sounds.

Grafman gestured impatiently. "What is this, Webber, you going to be married to every note you write?"

Webber leaned back, contained fury narrowing his already small mouth, chocolate ice cream running down his fingers. "First the ballad, now this! Shit. They were the strongest numbers in the score!"

"Reynolds," the PA system boomed, "party of four." Mama, papa and two baby bears pushed their way into the restaurant.

"I don't really want this," Thea was saying, looking at her cone with faint distaste. "I think they mixed pistachio in with the strawberry. It's all yellow. Where can I get rid of it?"

Grafman held out a hand. "At the price they're charging, *I'll* eat it." He finished off what was left of his own.

Thea stood up, dangling car keys from her fingers. Her voice had lost its sparkle. "I'm ready to go. Come on, boys, I'll drop you off."

"Birds?" Grafman looked up at her speculatively. "You're going to spend the whole afternoon looking at birds?" With what seemed more like anger than playfulness he gave her naked thigh a small slap.

"Mi-itch!" The laugh was two descending notes, a minor third, the smile that went with it evaporated slowly as though her facial muscles were tired. "You're going to be working. You don't need me."

"I have to call New York," Grafman said, more to himself than anyone else, and turned to the two men. "We'll get together about four-thirty." Webber nodded glumly. Alvin inclined his head in agreement. "Okay, let's go." He stood up and Alvin followed suit.

Webber licked disconsolately at his sticky fingers. "I'll see you later," he said.

Grafman looked annoyed. "What are you going to do, *run* back? In this heat?"

Webber looked away.

Irritably, Grafman said, "It's *your* blood pressure," and set off after the others, chomping on Thea's ice cream.

"Rome. Party of one."

I went into the cheerful, clattering place, past the long soda fountain and the old-fashioned candy jars, and on into a room solidly reminiscent of ice cream parlors and simpler days. The shrimp and avocado salad seemed a long time coming, and I spent some time trying to decide whether "Alvin," the bland, boyish-faced man from the airport, and the avaricious Mr. Persky of the Ruskin-Webber conflict could be one and the same. But my heart wasn't in it. Aware that time was limited and the Refuge very large, I willed the waitress to hurry.

And finally set out for the Refuge with absolutely no idea that kismet had hitched a ride in my car.

CHAPTER SIX

I PASSED A SIGN ANNOUNCING THAT THE REFUGE WAS closed "from sundown to sunup," wondering how they determined the opening and closing on rainy days, and drove on between dense, bristling mangrove swamps. I looked for birds and saw none. Then the road began to wind between the banks of vast lagoons, sheets of blue-tinted pewter that stretched, infinitely serene, enduring, imperturbable, to distant, wraithlike strands of obscure vegetation. In the enormous, humid stillness the place seemed primordial.

Rounding a turn in the road I saw, parked just ahead, a green Chevy with a Tennessee license plate. An elderly man and woman in wash-and-wear slack suits stood nearby on the bank with field glasses trained on a peninsula of matted mangrove that jutted into the lagoon. I stopped behind the Chevy and joined them on the bank, holding my mother's binoculars and bird book.

"What is it?" I asked.

"Royal tern," the man said quietly.

I focused the glasses, moved them back and forth across the

tangle of branches out there across the water. "What's it look like?"

"Gray and white, red bill, black legs, black and white crown."

Patiently I scanned the branches, and saw nothing but luxuriant mangrove. The elderly couple departed. I fiddled with the focus and still couldn't see it. I decided he'd made up the whole thing. Determined to find something in that hushed and humid sanctuary, I walked up the road a bit and tried a different vantage point. Here at last I spotted a blue-and-white bird with a long, sinuous neck that the bird book identified as a Louisiana heron. Encouraged, I scanned further and found an orange-billed ibis. I was becoming quite excited at my prowess, moved across the roadway to the opposite lagoon, and discovered an elegant white egret, moving with great dignity through the water like a Queen Mother. I almost expected it to raise one wing in graceful salute as it passed.

I departed for the next observation post, driving at a snail's pace over the crushed coral roadway, scanning the branches of roadside trees and shrubs. For a while the vegetation took over and the lagoons became no more than canals on each side of the road, then the bushes and bracken gave way again and the vista opened to an immense span of water, its surface peppered to the horizon with birds. At a rough guess, a zillion. Never, surely, had so many birds congregated in the same place at the same time. It was as though there had been some celestial victory parade up there in the solar system, and they'd used birds instead of confetti. I dug out my fixed-lens camera (Elliot would never let me, unaccompanied, carry the one with the wide-angle and zoom and whatnot in separate cases) and took a few shots, knowing that no little box I wielded could ever capture this lavish spectacle.

The bank here was flat and grassy. I took a path that followed the curve of the water away from the road for several hundred yards and, rounding a clump of bushes, stopped, blinked, gaped, and murmured, "Jesus!" There before me, perched on a log, was a piano keyboard!

A bird, actually, with its huge wings spread, a large black bird with a yellowish bill, its head and the back of its snaky neck spiky with quills. But the white wings, spread out as though for flight, were marked with black and looked exactly like a piano keyboard. I groped for the bird book and found I'd left it in the car.

Will Greenfield believe me, I wondered, when I tell him I saw a piano bird?

I aimed the camera, praying the bird would sit still while I focused. It sat there, all right, but folded its wings at the very instant the shutter clicked.

"Spread your wings, dammit!" The bird turned its head away disdainfully, presenting me with a black blob. "Please," I cajoled. The bird graciously spread its wings. And flew away. Greenfield would never believe me.

I returned to the car, looked in vain for the bird book, hoped I'd dropped it in the trunk when I'd gone for the camera, and drove on between the banks where tiny white daisy-like flowers dotted the verge on either side, past a tall cabbage palm like some tribal medicine man, its top a headdress, its long trunk wearing a ceremonial robe of shaggy dead fronds, past a cream-colored station wagon stopped beside one of the canals apparently only for mother to administer first aid to a small girl with a bloody nose. Eventually I came to another lagoon, this one with an observation tower of wooden posts like a gazebo on stilts.

There was a car pulled up on the bank. A pale-blue Dodge. I was surprised. Sarah McChesney had so convinced me of Thea's ulterior motive in mentioning the Refuge that it never occurred to me I'd see her here, actually watching birds. Or had she already picked up her quarry and brought him here for what Greenfield would call dalliance? I looked around and saw the tomato-red shorts and white shirt carefully descending the stairway from the top of the tower, alone. No Leroy in the vicinity that I could see.

I started for the tower and halfway there we passed, eyeing each other. She gave me a faint smile. I had the feeling she knew we'd met before but couldn't remember where. Probably thinks I'm the hotel chambermaid, I thought. I had one foot on the lookout stairway when I heard her cry out, "Oh *no!*" and looked back. "No! No!" She was tugging desperately at the door of the blue Dodge.

"I'm locked out!" she called to me. I went back. She kept

pulling uselessly at the door. "The keys are inside. But I didn't push the lock when I got out. I didn't. I know I didn't." Her classic forehead and delicate upper lip were gleaming with perspiration and one hand clutched at the front of her shirt as though she were going to be sick. She was upset out of all proportion to the gravity of the situation.

"Well, let's see—" I said.

I was not unfamiliar with the predicament, having found myself in it once while parked briefly in a tow-away zone in Manhattan and once in a thunderstorm in Maine.

"I put on the air conditioning," she said sluggishly, "all the windows are up." She leaned against the car, abandoned to hopelessness.

I looked into the car. A patchwork carryall sat brightly on the front seat, a large striped beach rug lay crumpled in the back. I walked around the car looking closely at the windows and found a quarter-inch crack at the top of one in the rear. "I think we could get something through here," I said. "Let's hope my mother left a coat hanger in the trunk." I opened the trunk of the Ford: one small folding beach chair, one half-gallon bottle of water (did she expect to be stranded in a desert?), a turquoise towel, neatly folded, a pair of rubber thongs. No coat hanger, no piece of wire, no length of rope, no ball of twine. Ah, there was the bird book! "Nothing useful here." I shut the trunk.

"I didn't lock it," she said to herself, like someone refusing to believe she had touched the vase that lies smashed on the floor. "I didn't. Oh God, if it had to happen why didn't it happen before, when I went back to the room, where the spare keys are."

"Are you alone?" My euphemism for "Is Leroy around, or expected?"

She turned to me with an unfocused, disoriented look.

"Did you come here with someone?"

She shook her head. She looked, suddenly, beyond caring. All her accustomed radiance, the ultramagnetic field in which she moved by virtue of physical beauty, seemed to have been neutralized. She was only a forlorn figure with corn-yellow hair who didn't feel so good.

"We'll have to get help," I said. I looked up and down the empty roadway. "You'd think there'd be more people around.

Maybe it's too hot, or they all came earlier in the day. In any case there's a green Chevy up ahead somewhere, and I passed a station wagon a few minutes ago. I'll go back to the station wagon, you look up ahead. Somebody's bound to have something we can use.''

She pushed herself away from the car, wiped her forehead with the back of one hand and started off haltingly down the road, weaving a little. Either the theatrical instinct has taken over, I thought, or the heat's gotten to her.

I left my car where it was. Once you started on this road there was no turning back, the road was one-way, a loop that emerged, at the end of the Refuge drive, higher up the Sanibel–Captiva road. The station wagon couldn't be that far away.

A half-mile farther on I still hadn't seen it. They could have tired of bird-watching, I supposed, or become physically weary and gone back to their rooms for a nap, just driven by me unnoticed while I was busy with the camera. It was very hot; even my thin Indian cotton skirt and shirt were sticking damply to my back and legs. I was tempted to give up, but trudged nobly on, telling myself I'd go as far as the next bend in the road and if there was nothing there turn back. There was something there, but not the station wagon. A white Toyota from Illinois. A stocky, balding man in his sixties stood by the car gazing through binoculars at a high branch of a tree across the road, a matronly woman in a print dress beside him squinting in the same direction.

I apologized for interrupting and described my plight, or, rather, Thea's. The man was delighted, smiling all over his sunburned dumpling of a face as though he were in for a treat. He unlocked a trunk that held a promising jumble of tools, boxes, and odds and ends.

"Ha!" he said, "you picked the right fella, young lady. I used to do this for a living."

"Open locked cars?" I looked at him warily.

"Used to be on the force. A cop. You wouldn't believe the number of people who lock themselves out of their cars." He came up with a black metal hanger and a pair of pliers and proceeded to untwist the neck of the hanger. "You wait here, Dotty, I'll be right back."

I protested that I didn't want to trouble him further—if I

could just have the hanger we'd manage the rest—but he wouldn't be cheated out of his fun. As we started back up the road, I wondered if Thea had been successful and already had the car unlocked. My man kept working on the hanger, and by the time we came in sight of the cars he had a three-foot length of more or less unbent wire, at the end of which he was fashioning a small loop.

Thea's car was still locked, the keys still dangling from the ignition, and Thea was nowhere in sight. I thought of going to find her, but it was possible this man and his hanger wouldn't do the trick and in the meantime she might just run into a locksmith who carried his tools with him. Or a burglar.

My friend the ex-cop was ever so carefully letting the looped end of the wire down the inside of the window toward the lock. There! No. The angle of the wire wasn't sharp enough, the loop dangled a half-inch away from the lock. He withdrew the wire, bent it, inserted it once more through the crack, let it down. . . . It took four revisions of the angle before the wire reached its object. Finally the loop went over the knob and very, very slowly he pulled up on the wire. . . .

"Damn!" he swore softly. The loop had skidded up over the knob without pulling it. The circumference of the loop was too large. He withdrew the wire, used the pliers to tighten the loop and went through the whole slow, agonizing procedure again. Now the loop was too small. He withdrew the wire. . . .

I looked down the road for a sign of red shorts and white shirt. Nothing. How far had she gone?

"Got it!" His red face beaming at me, he opened the car door by the handle.

"Oh! Wonderful! Thank you *so* much!"

He bent the length of wire into thirds. "Nothing to it. Used to finagle those locks by the dozen."

"Well, we certainly appreciate it—"

"Be careful now. Keep those keys in your purse."

"Yes. Thanks again."

He went off down the road. What now? Wait, obviously. A maroon Buick came along and pulled up behind my car. Three women, two hearty and middle-aged, one frail, white-haired and cranky, made their way foot by slow foot toward the observation tower, each of the younger ones supporting an elbow of the octogenarian.

I decided to visit the observation tower, with my binoculars. When I got to the top I ignored the lagoon and focused on the road. There wasn't much to see, a quarter-mile of empty winding road skirting the lagoon and disappearing around a bend. After a while I watched the birds wheeling and flapping and settling and making a racket with their woodnotes wild—screech, croak, caw, crow, honk, hoot. The two middle-aged women in their print dresses came up the stairway and I went down, stepping around the old lady, who sat at the bottom.

I went back to the car. I took some shots of the bird-strewn water. I walked up the road a short distance, to the next bend. A gray Volvo drove by, quickly. Florida plates, for heaven's sake. Whatever happened to Wyoming and Alaska? I realized I was out of sight of the cars and went back. It was now over an hour since Thea and I had separated to look for help. Had she gotten a lift into town? To buy a hanger? To call Grafman to bring the extra keys? To get one of the crew to come back with her? I couldn't stay here indefinitely. I couldn't go off and leave her car there, unlocked, with the keys dangling.

Finally I wrote a note on a postcard I'd bought to send to the Olivers, pinned it to the windshield with one of the wipers, took the keys and Thea's bag, locked the car, got into my mother's Ford, and left. I would go to The Gulls, ask for Mr. Grafman— let's hope that really is his name—and if she wasn't there already, tell him what was going on. Let him take it from there. I wound my way out of the Refuge and turned down the San–Cap road. As I approached the intersection with Periwinkle Way I saw a bicyclist wobbling down the bicycle path up ahead, also heading for Periwinkle. I passed the bicycle, pulled off the road, got out of the car and waved both hands urgently at Sherman Ruskin. He saw me and ran into a palm tree.

CHAPTER SEVEN

WHEN I REACHED RUSKIN HE WAS SITTING WITH HIS back against the tree, his legs straight out in front of him, cushioned by the prostrate bicycle, his eyes resting thoughtfully on the far horizon.

" 'You're too sedentary, Ruskin,' " he quoted from some recent encounter, " 'Get more exercise. Buy a bicycle.' Hypocritical fucking internist. Rides around in a golf cart."

"Are you hurt?"

"Probably."

"Should I go for help?" I was beginning to regret ever having seen him and all his adversaries.

He considered my offer, then leaned to one side, put his hands flat on the ground, crawled away from the bicycle and stood up, brushing off his Bermudas, a fresh pair today, tan-and-black plaid. "What was all that semaphoring about?"

"You're sure nothing's broken?"

"Of *course* things are broken. My spirit. My dreams. Who are you, anyway? You've been following me. On the beach. In the pool. My wife sent you down to check on me, right? No. If she hired a snoop it would be a Japanese wrestler. Very careful

47

woman. Takes very few chances. Carries two umbrellas. Who did you say you were?"

"My mother lives in the apartment next to yours. Your parents'. I need to find the man who—I'm not certain about his name—he's staying at The Gulls, I think, with a very attractive blond woman—you and your friend were watching her on the beach. The man has a gray Vandyke. I *think* her name is Thea."

He peered at me over the rims of his sunglasses. "You always incoherent like this?"

"It's an incoherent situation. Do you know who I mean?"

"Grafman?"

"Possibly. The name has been mentioned. The point is, the girl—woman—Thea, if that's her name—was locked out of her car. We separated to look for help, and she hasn't come back." I gestured behind me. "In the Refuge. I have her car keys. I was on my way to The Gulls to see if she—could you just tell me her name?—or his name? I don't know whom to ask for."

"Whom?" He leaned toward me in an excess of astonishment. "Did you say *whom*? In your incoherent condition?"

"I've had rigorous training," I said, thinking of Greenfield.

He nodded sadly, as though he'd feared as much, and looked down at the bicycle lying in the dust. "How about giving me a lift?"

"To The Gulls? Because that's where I'm going."

"To The Gulls, what do I care. Just so I don't have to pedal that thing."

"Well—if we can fit it into the car. Where's your orange flag?"

"It got knocked off by a vicious fence."

Ruskin's mechanical skills were on a par with his athletic prowess and mine were never anything to rave about. After much sweating and straining, with one wheel still half out of the trunk, we secured the lid as best we could with cord borrowed from the gas station down the road, and I drove off.

Ruskin leaned his head against the back of the passenger seat, the peak of his cap slipping over his eyes. "I think I'll stay in the car while you deliver your message. Grafman and I are not on the best of terms. A little matter of shrewd insight on my part and obstinate stupidity on his. Producers, as has been noted in story and legend since Aristophanes, are congenitally myopic.''

''What's he producing?''

''Something that began as a musical and will inevitably end as sewage.''

''My mother tells me you're a writer.''

''Too bad. I was hoping to pass myself off as a movie star. How do you feel about writers?''

''Which ones?''

He raised one hand in surrender. ''A literate female. Just my luck.''

''I gather you wrote this musical?''

''Nobody *writes* a musical. A musical is a group of unrelated goals that *collide*, like a seven-car pileup on the New Jersey Turnpike. Somebody comes up with a book. Somebody else comes up with a score. A producer comes in and destroys half the book and a third of the score. Director comes in and destroys the rest. Choreographer arrives and wants to cut out everything but the dancing. And that's the *good* part. The real trouble starts when the star decides he or she really wants to do a different story in a different locale with a different writer, director, composer, choreographer and cast. War is declared, everyone goes to his battle station, and when it's all over, the debris is served up on Broadway as a musical.''

''Sounds like a grueling undertaking. Why did you decide to do it?''

''I don't know. Maybe it was nostalgia. I thought it would be nice to have one last show on Broadway where the boys were sleeping with the girls.''

We reached an intersection to the left of which lay the Sea Grape Inn. I turned right and eventually saw the looming sugar cubes that made up The Gulls. The main entrance was predictable: glass and brass and stiff pruned bushes. ''In case she's here,'' I said, ''and he isn't, I assume they're sharing an apartment under his name?''

''You betcha. C 12.''

''And her last name? In case I have to use it?''

''Quinn. Thea Quinn. From Minnesota by way of regional theater and an Off-Broadway revue to Mitchell Grafman's flinty heart. A nice girl. Probably makes a good, wholesome mistress. Mayonnaise sandwiches by the fire at the end of a hard day. Cornflakes and orange juice at the end of a hard night. A real Rodgers and Hammerstein girl, if that's what you're looking for. You wouldn't think she'd be Grafman's type.'' He shook his head in wonderment. ''He's crazy-nuts for her. Obsessed. Bananas.''

I left him sitting there, the cap still over his eyes, and went in search of C 12. It was on the ground floor at the far end of one of the sugar cubes. Down an outdoor corridor punctuated by the occasional numbered door, the muted sound of a live piano came to greet me. A delicate melody, tenderly played. Could that be Webber, the aggressive Terrier? Given his hot defense of ''the score'' while dripping ice cream, I assumed he must be the composer in this crew. The ring of a telephone interrupted the performance and the sweet, plaintive notes trickled off as I reached the door. I knocked, the door opened, and there he was: Richard Wagner in jogging shoes. Scowling and pugnacious on the outside, ''Liebestod'' within.

Beyond him lay a living room awash in palm-tree-printed chintz, with a Yamaha upright squeezed between one end of a sofa and the sliding glass doors leading to the balcony. In a large, palmy armchair Grafman lounged, naked from the waist up, speaking into the telephone, a cigarillo burning between his fingers. On the sofa sat ''Alvin'' from the airport, a script in a blue binder on his lap, a small smile on his lips as he gazed out at the balcony.

''I'm looking for Thea Quinn,'' I said.

''She's not here.'' Webber looked flushed and sweaty.

''Have you heard from her in the last hour?''

''What is it? Who's that?'' Grafman called out, one hand over the mouthpiece.

''She wants to know if you heard from Thea.''

''What do you mean? Bring her in. Wait a minute, will you?'' This last, presumably, to me and he resumed his phone conversation. ''Sandy, listen to me, last week we did thirty-six percent capacity, that's not going to send anybody's kid to college. I'm not interested in break-even points—I'm not interested in meeting the operating costs—this is not a philanthropic gesture—''

Webber had motioned me into the apartment and shut the

door, and I stood there on the teal-blue carpeting with Thea's car keys in my hand while Grafman carried on, his words rude but his manner mild.

"Shut up a minute and listen, to hell with word of mouth, I want to post that notice, we can always take it down if—I'll worry about their morale some other time—why don't you get yourself on a plane to London and take a look at that National Theater megillah. And take the airline with the discount fare. If it's worth a trip let me know. No. Post it! Good-bye, I'm in a meeting." He dropped the phone into its cradle and said, "What happened to Thea?"

"I didn't say anything happened to her," I pointed out. "I'm just trying to find her." As concisely as possible, I related the events of the past hour and a half while Webber paced the room, perspiring freely into his green polo shirt, running his hands through his mop of brown sheep's-wool hair, and Alvin watched me remotely.

Grafman extinguished the cigarillo in a glass ashtray. He had a calculating face, publicly amiable, privately immune to any need or prerogative but its own. He heard me out with an expression that was impassive and suggested that a great deal of quick thinking was going on behind it.

"Crazy bitch," he muttered, standing and taking Thea's car keys from my outstretched hand. "*Had* to go look at some goddam flamingos. Gary, call a cab, look it up in the book." He crossed the living room and disappeared down a hallway.

"What are you going to do?" Webber called after him. "You want me to come with you? Where would we look for her, it's a frigging big place. Maybe I should stay here and work with Alvin." Alvin meanwhile had unearthed a telephone directory and was looking carefully through the pages. Webber put out a hand for the book, withdrew the hand, ran it through his hair, eyed me nervously, said "Christ, I really needed this!" turned away, turned back, said to me, "How did you know where to bring the keys?"

That was a long story. I cut it short. "I happened to run into Mr. Ruskin."

"Ruskin!" Speculation, curiosity, bewilderment, all leaped about in his eyes. Alvin, having dialed a number, handed him the telephone receiver and he said, "Uh—hello—we need a cab. The Gulls—"

Alvin gave me a small polite smile and repaired to the balcony, where he stood looking into the distance. I turned to go, but Webber waved a hand to stop me. "Grafman. Five minutes? Okay." He replaced the phone, crossed the room with his quick, impatient, marathon-walker gait and helped himself to ice cubes from a bucket that stood on a Formica-topped bar wagon against the wall. "What do you think happened? I mean, how did you and Thea—you're a friend of Sherman's?"

"No, I'm staying in the apartment next door to his." As an explanation it left a good deal to be desired—about six paragraphs—but Webber's mind did not seem to be traveling in a straight line.

"She's probably standing there waiting," he said, pouring soda from a bottle into the glass of ice cubes. Three other bottles stood beside the ice bucket, all of them soda. Not a sherry, bourbon or white wine among them. Gracious living was apparently not high on Grafman's list of priorities. "Hanging around the car, waiting," he repeated, but without conviction. Belatedly he noticed the glass in his hand and courtesy came struggling up through his preoccupations. "Drink?"

I shook my head, said I really had to go, and opened the apartment door to find Sherman Ruskin standing there in all his knobby-kneed glory, one fist raised and about to knock.

"They wanted me to move the car," he said, "but I'm not as strong as I used to be."

I looked at the ring of car keys decorating the middle finger of my left hand. "Force of habit, sorry. I'm leaving anyway. Do you want a ride back to the Sea Grape, or—?"

"Sherm!" Webber had trotted over, rattling ice cubes. "Were you there? Did you see Thea? Were you in the bird preserve?"

"Why would I be there? I've seen feathers before." He gestured around the room. "So neat? I expected to see the place littered with creative pages."

Grafman reappeared, pulling on a fresh sport shirt in a muted blue plaid. His eyes flicked over Ruskin. "Oh, it's the quitter. What happened, you change your mind?"

"Goodness gracious," Ruskin said, "that course of action never occurred to me."

"You know what's wrong with writers?" Grafman buttoned the two bottom buttons, leaving the gray chest curls open to the breeze. "They don't stay hungry long enough."

"You've got it wrong, Mitch. The appetite's always there, it just gets refined. You can't tempt a beef Wellington man with frozen pizza."

Webber choked on a mouthful of soda.

"So what're you doing here?" Grafman demanded.

"This woman picked me up."

Grafman glanced at me to see if he'd missed something, decided he hadn't and called out to the balcony, "Alvin, if we're not back in an hour, I'll call you. Gary, you come with me."

"I thought I'd stay here and—"

"Drink up and let's go."

Webber put his glass on the coffee table. "I've had enough."

Grafman glanced pointedly at the glass half full of soda. "*You* buy the next bottle." His hand on the door, he gestured us all out.

"Mind if I use your john, Mitch? I'll leave with this lady immediately afterwards." Without waiting for a reply, Ruskin went toward the rear of the apartment.

Grafman hesitated, then went out the door.

Webber followed him, calling over his shoulder, "Think about that, Alvin. About the setup for *Rape and Ransom*—"

I had no desire to join those two in the elevator and waited, in the open doorway, for Ruskin to come back. Alvin had come in from the balcony. He gave me his polite smile, a smile that seemed to exist without any help from him, without any parting of the lips, as though the corners of the mouth were being pulled up by some hidden puppeteer. He seemed shy, and a little overwhelmed by the high-voltage personalities around him.

"Sorry to be in the way," I said.

"Not at all," he whispered hoarsely. "I was watching a plover on the beach."

His quiet good manners were something of a relief after the hectic, self-centered behavior of the others. If this were indeed the infamous Persky, I couldn't help wondering what the other half of the story might be. What, for instance, had Ruskin done to provoke this man into making unreasonable demands? It was difficult not to like Ruskin, but that didn't make him a saint. Confronted with Alvin's reserved and vulnerable face, I found myself marginally less sympathetic to Ruskin's plight.

Alvin picked up Webber's half-full glass of soda, carried it around a waist-high partition into the kitchen area and came back just as Ruskin returned, with his long, heavy lope, creased Bermudas, lank hair and nasal voice.

"So," he said conversationally to Alvin, "how's good old Rodeo Drive? Any humans show up there yet? No, huh? Just the same old Maseratis and like that?" He clucked in sympathy. "To think of all those wagon trains a hundred years ago, setting out for the orange groves, with such high hopes. Tell me—that series you were writing for, out there—about the beachcombers—I caught one of the episodes but I missed the credits. Who directed it?"

For a moment there was no reply, only the smile. Then Alvin croaked, "Why do you ask?"

"I was wondering if he was a foot fetishist or a failed podiatrist. I never saw so many close-ups of bare toes and insteps. Must have been quite a challenge, writing dialogue for feet."

Alvin seemed to take no offense at this. The smile stayed in place.

I moved toward the corridor. "I think we should—"

"Sure." Ruskin took a step in my direction. "We'll leave you now, Mr. Persky"—he gestured at the blue binder on the coffee table—"to get on with your dismembering."

I went down the corridor, Ruskin at my heels. So. *Alvin* was the demanding Mr. Persky.

"Likable fellow," Ruskin said as we waited for the elevator. "Nice and quiet. One might almost say comatose."

"He's involved in this—production?"

"Contractually, not yet." He held the elevator door while I stepped in. Knighthood still flowered. "But the terms, as they say, have been negotiated. Nothing fancy. He asked for the moon, the sun and a few space stations, and he got them. They think cosmic in cut-throat country."

All this needling, I thought. All these blistering comments. Ruskin seemed innocuous enough: a gangling man, with no muscle tone to speak of, who would probably not last two minutes in a fight with a three-year-old. But rage bubbled incessantly, just under the surface. I wondered if this was par for the course when there was a show-business power struggle going on. With my limited knowledge of theatrical business arrangements, the scraps of talk I'd heard over the last few days gave me only the haziest notion of what was actually at stake.

In the car, making our way back along Gulf Drive to the Sea Grape, I ventured a question.

"I always thought musicals were put together in smoke-filled offices in Manhattan. Is there some reason you're all working down here on the island?"

"My fault. All my fault. Paid my folks a visit two years ago, got drunk on unaccustomed relaxation, and when I got back to New York, I made the mistake of mentioning to my agent that there could be a musical in the Gasparilla legend. Never tell an agent anything. Keep conversations to a minimum. Hello, where's my check, good-bye. Anything more and before you know it you're embroiled. 'Pirates!' he said, 'what a great idea! These things are cyclical, it's just about time for a buccaneer revival!' And before I could find a friend to give me an alternative assignment, there I was, making a suicide pact with Gary Webber to work on a musical about Gasparilla."

"And Gasparilla, I gather, had something to do with this island?"

"Don't you know the history of this place?"

"Only up to Ponce de León. I fell asleep halfway down page twenty-nine."

"Well, keep going, it gets better."

"So you all congregated here to pick up local color for the production."

"We came here because Grafman came here and he came here because Thea wanted to. 'It could fill in the background for me,' she said, and Grafman, who thinks of himself as William Randolph Hearst, said, "Sure, Marion,' and ordered us all down here. He's going to build her a house, can you believe it? On Captiva. Wait until his two ex-wives hear about it. Middle age is a very, very dangerous time of life."

We turned in to the Sea Grape parking lot, untied the rope

that held the trunk lid down, and removed Ruskin's bicycle. He looked down at it with great dislike.

"I'd take it back," he said, "but I paid two weeks' rent. Grafman's parsimony is rubbing off on me. That man"—he trundled the bike up the stairs to the landing—"is a study in schizophrenia. I've seen him go ten miles out of his way to save three cents on a gallon of gas. I've seen him come close to cardiac arrest because his secretary bought a new typewriter ribbon while the old one was still legible. But Thea only has to say she's cold and he flies her to Martinique for the weekend." He chained the bike to the railing, then turned to me with a businesslike frown. "So. You want to have an affair, or not?"

I bit back a laugh. There was only one way to handle that. "Where and when?"

"Oy," he said, and went to the door of his apartment.

CHAPTER EIGHT

T HE PATIENT, BENT DOUBLE AND CLUTCHING THE WALL, made her precarious way toward the dining alcove.

"Do you really know what you're doing?" I asked fearfully.

"It's just logic," she panted. "If I keep *lying* there, I could be getting better and neither one of us would know it. I have to *experiment.*"

"Is that what Dr. Cole said?"

"Oh, Dr. Cole," she dismissed him.

"Well? How does it feel? Does it hurt?"

"Of *course* it hurts. I'm *tense.* Tension causes *pain.*"

"But is it the pain of the *tension,* or the *old* pain?"

"It's *pain.*"

"Try not being tense."

"Easy to say!" She was getting snappish: was that a sign of health, or a rage at her condition? It seemed to me I detected a comparative ease of movement and told her so.

"Oh yes. Maybe I'll take up ballet," she gasped, reaching the dining room chair, lowering herself into it, and closing her eyes. The skin of her face in the overhead light, I noticed, was soft and powdery, and latticed with minute lines. There is always a time when you first realize that a parent is old, and the bottom drops out of your heart.

I blinked away the sting in my eyes, dished out dinner, entertained her with an account of the day's events. She enjoyed the story even more than the lamb chops and parsleyed rice, and when she was back in bed and I was stacking the dishes in the dishwasher, she was still dwelling on it.

"You know what *I* think?" she called out to me, "I think that blond girl *did* have an arrangement to meet the boy from the marina. At the Refuge. And when she went to look for help, she met him on his way to keep the date. And—"

"She was going in the wrong direction for that. She went toward the exit end of the Refuge. And any car going by would have passed me. I'd have seen him." And then I remembered the gray Volvo. I'd been too busy being surprised at the Florida plates to notice who was in the car.

"*And,*" my mother went on firmly, "that other girl was lying in wait, the botanist, with her camera, and the blonde and her *amour* caught her taking pictures and went after her to get the film back."

"That sounds familiar. Ray Milland. Or Joseph Cotten. Or Rosalind Russell. I think they stopped making that one in the fifties."

Still, I thought, life does have this adolescent habit of imitating old movies. International playgirls and wives of diplomats did occasionally turn on photographers and journalists with vengeance in their eyes. Suppose Thea *had* met Mr. Muscle. Suppose they *had* caught Sarah clicking her camera shutter, and had her at bay somewhere, trying to make her give up the "evidence."

But no, even granting that Leroy appearing on the scene was possible, why wouldn't Thea come back to the car first? Easy enough to get rid of me: "I found someone who's going to unlock the car for me, thanks so much, you don't have to wait." Whatever else she was, Thea was not featherbrained, she wouldn't take off for any prolonged activity knowing I was at the car, waiting.

Unless, of course, she had no control over the situation. Leroy looked single-minded enough and, God knows, strong enough, to do whatever he had the impulse to do, whenever the mood took him.

And the fact was, Thea had *not* come back to the car in the hour I was there.

The more I thought about it, the more it seemed that Sarah's little scheme, if she actually went through with it, could very well put her in jeopardy. Blackmail—and it was certainly a form of that—was not an occupation designed to endear the practitioner to his or her victim. Those old movies were strewn with discovered blackmailers in a state of rigor mortis. Oh Sarah, you nut, don't try it!

I took the kitchen garbage out to the communal dumpster.

Evening had descended; moist, warm, blue-black. Around the deserted swimming pool the lamps were lit, glowing amber globes sending their reflections snaking down into the dark water. Dusky palms stirred languidly, silhouetted against the indigo sky. From a window here and there a glint of saffron light gleamed around the edges of drawn venetian blinds. The sun-worshippers were resting from their arduous day's pursuit of pleasure. Where was Sarah? Safely at home among her joewood and inkberry and the varnish-smelling tea made from leaves of a gumbo-limbo, probably. Probably.

I went back up to the apartment, found the local telephone book tucked away under the kitchen counter with the colander and the griddle, looked up McChesney—there was only one— and dialed. After twelve rings I replaced the receiver. She could be out visiting a friend, having a late dinner in some restaurant, attending the Island Cinema.

I looked in on the invalid, watching a portable television set fitted out with an extension cord that stood by the foot of the bed on a ladder borrowed from the maintenance office. Something about a glamorous television anchorwoman and a man who was trying to discredit her. According to television, an ordinary reporter was a thing of the past: today you were an anchorperson with an extensive wardrobe or you were nothing. I found my *History of the Islands* and was about to settle down with it when the phone rang. My mother picked it up on the bedroom extension. I heard her conversing and flipped through the book to find the chapter on Gasparilla.

"Maggie!" she called after a few minutes. "It's Elliot!"

Elliot? From *Lima*? And she was *chatting*? I grabbed the phone.

"Elliot!"

"I got your message via the telex from the office. Delia sounds in good spirits."

"She's improving. How are *you*?"

He was fine, a little gastric distress from eating salad, the people at the Lima office were treating him royally, there were armed guards on the streets, mostly in front of banks, nothing frightening, he was going down to the site the following day, the men down there had been working by cookbook rules, their stress analysis was off, he'd have to examine their assumptions, if he made it to Cuzco he would get me a poncho.

And he was gone. Cuzco, I thought. Dun-colored mountains, shaggy llamas, stony-eyed, barefoot Indian women poorer than poor, with their woven wares spread on the ground, haggling over prices. One should have to spend months on horseback to get there, to arrive, finally, among the dusty, ageless Incan artifacts. It was a kind of blasphemy to swoop down in a jet.

I heard my mother saying something over the aggressive inanities of a commercial and went down the hall to her room.

"I said *what* is Elliot doing down there?"

"Being a consultant. They want to put up some low-cost housing and it has to be made from prestressed concrete, they don't have anything but sand down there, it's a desert. The concrete has to be manufactured to certain specifications and Elliot analyzes the specifications and . . . um . . . he's going to bring me a Peruvian poncho."

"Is it *safe* down there?"

"Is it safe anywhere?"

She turned back to her anchorwoman. She didn't want to hear that kind of talk. I went back to the living room with my *History:* she wasn't the only one who sought escape. Curled up on the sofa, I opened the book and the phone rang again. This time, Greenfield.

"The Greek," he said, referring to Calli Dohanis who did the *Reporter*'s layout, "has come down with the flu. I think she may have passed it on to Deutsch." (Helen, who presided over the Varityper and the Justo-writer.) "There are tissue boxes all over the place. The Greek says she will die if she has to come in tomorrow, I've told her she will die if she doesn't. As of Thursday I will be without staff, except for Klein.'' (Stewart, junior reporter, except in his own mind, where he was at least another Henry Luce.) ''And Klein's journalistic style, as you well know, makes *Ulysses* seem a model of clarity. When are you coming back?''

I told him there was cause for optimism, the patient seemed to be recuperating, and if the recovery continued apace I could think about returning on the weekend.

''*Think* about it?'' he said. ''Going home is hardly a decision on a par with committing yourself to a polar expedition.''

''I'm not so sure about that. What's the temperature up there?'' The silence at the other end suggested such calamitous shock that I quickly added, ''I'll be back, I'll be back. On the weekend.''

More to have the last word than because he thought it probable, he said, ''Friday would be better.''

I settled down, at last, with *The History of the Islands* to find out about Gasparilla.

A notorious buccaneer, was Gasparilla. Had been an admiral of the Spanish Fleet until he stole the crown jewels, took off in one of the Navy's ships, and set up pirate headquarters in the islands, living in regal splendor with a harem of female prisoners garnered from passing vessels. Fidelity was not his strong suit and he was easily bored; whenever he tired of a particular female she suffered a premature death and was replaced by another. Sort of a Spanish spoiled kid with too many toys.

Then comeuppance sailed into his life on board one of the vessels he captured: a Spanish princess who, with a clutch of Mexican Indian girls, was en route to Spain for religious education. Gasparilla turned over the Mexican girls to his randy crew, but the princess was another matter. He found himself in thrall to her. No flinging her onto the silken couch, no casual ravishment of her person. The princess was treated like a queen. And like a queen, she snubbed him, inflaming his ardor. He importuned. She rejected. He persisted. She remained an invulnerable fortress. The man was obsessed with her, mad with desire, then finally just plain mad. In a fury of frustration he went at her with his cutlass and severed the lovely head from the luscious body. Then, possibly haunted by her memory, or filled with remorse, or possibly just tired of the endless round of seduction and decapitation, he went out on deck, wrapped an anchor chain around his legs and threw himself into the waters off the island of Captiva, where she was buried.

"Ha!" I said.

I closed the book, turned off the lamp and went out onto the balcony. In a half-hour it would be midnight. The island slept in a hushed, balmy darkness. Beyond the pebbled path that led to the beach a small strip of sand was visible, silvered by an unseen moon and washed by the darkly glimmering Gulf. A scented breeze, humid, seductive, stirred the night air briefly. All that broke the deep silence was the soft clattering of palm fronds brushing against each other, like rain pattering on a tin roof.

Pirates on this island? Swashbucklers, cutthroats, plundering passing ships? Holding women for ransom in cabins made of saw-palmetto logs? Captives on Captiva? Why not—1782, after all. Some of it could have happened. Or all of it. From a twentieth-century vantage point it might seem improbable and stagy, but who's to say that if Gasparilla and his men had been given a glimpse of the future, they might not have felt they could learn a piratical thing or two from current practices?

I took a deep breath of warm air heavy with the fragrance of flowers.

Was it too late at night to telephone a casual acquaintance?

I could hang up immediately on hearing her voice: Sorry, wrong number.

I took the phone out to the balcony to avoid waking my mother, dialed, waited. There was no answer at the other end.

CHAPTER NINE

DAYLIGHT APPLIED ITS CUSTOMARY WASH OF SANITY TO the forebodings of the night before. With my orange juice I convinced myself that Sarah was doing her morning chores in the garden. Over coffee and blueberry muffin I imagined her riding her bike blithely along the San–Cap road to her work at the Conservation Center. By the time I went down to the Sea Grape office to collect the mail, I had all but banished her from my thoughts.

There was a letter for my mother from a friend in Boston, a notice from the local chapter of the Audubon Society of an imminent lecture at the Community Center, the latest issue of *Stately Homes*, a periodical to which she had once subscribed in a fit of Anglophilia, and a bill from Dr. Cole. I handed them over and asked how she wanted to spend the morning. The maid service provided by Housekeeping, she said, would be coming to clean the apartment, why didn't I go out for a while, go to the lighthouse, that would give me a nice long walk on the beach.

It was not a good day for walking on the beach; the weather had turned cool and blowy, with scudding clouds that obscured the sun for long stretches. I thought I might go back to the Refuge and finish the tour Thea had interrupted. (Not so much as an apology, either, I noted, or an explanation as to why she'd left me standing there. Possibly she already had the celebrity's self-involvement that takes other people's services for granted. So much for carefully including my telephone number on the card I had slipped under her windshield wiper.)

I drove out to the San–Cap road; turned onto it, and a few minutes later noticed, on the left, the entrance to the Conservation Center. What the hell, I thought, it was open to the public, I was the public. I turned in and followed the bumpy road to where a few cars were parked. A sign on a large bin of free coconuts said ONE PER FAMILY. A nice touch, both friendly and, in the spirit of the place, careful not to exhaust natural resources.

It was a short climb from the parking lot to the one-story building that housed the center's office. At the window that dispensed tickets for guided tours of the grounds I asked where I could find Sarah McChesney. A clerical face suggested that I ask at the office across the floor, and the young man at the desk behind the office door said, "Sarah? I haven't seen her today. She's probably at the nursery. That's down below, just to the right of the parking space."

Back I went, wandered a bit, discovered a rather inconspicuous sign pointing to the nursery, and a little farther on, a woman, squatting before a potted wild-olive seedling on a long narrow path. On each side of the path hundreds of potted plants in various stages of primary growth sat on the bare ground in orderly rows, each with its own name tag. A kind of botanical sleep-away camp.

The woman, looking up with a pleasant smile, said, "Sarah? I haven't seen her today. She may be up at the office."

"They said she was probably down here."

"No," she said cheerfully, "she isn't."

"Do you expect her?"

"Oh yes. She's usually here by now. Can I help you with something?"

"I—um—no, thanks. Not important."

I went back to the car, drove on to the Refuge. People are often delayed, for no important reason. Flat tire. Faulty alarm clock. Long line at the bank. On the other hand, it wasn't that far to Captiva, I could . . . No. This was becoming obsessive. I drove into the Refuge entrance.

Passing by all the points of interest I'd already seen, I stopped finally where a Datsun with Iowa license plates was parked, and joined a group of three women and two men standing by a canal looking down at the water. It took me a few minutes to make out the immobile family of alligators: mother (not father, father alligators saw no essential difference between their offspring and a good three-decker sandwich, so mom kept him away) and three—no, four—no, five—baby alligators. They were smaller than I'd expected and not terribly interesting. I moved on, came upon a gallinule—obviously a Bible-reading bird—who was running *on top* of the water as he worked up to takeoff speed before soaring into the air. Farther on, an osprey swooped down on a lagoon, its predatory eye on some unwary fish.

Toward the end of the Refuge road a signpost, illegible from the car, seemed to mark the entrance to a footpath through the mangrove jungle. I parked and went to investigate. THE GASPA-RILLA TRAIL, the sign announced. NAMED AFTER THE PIRATE WHO CAME TO THESE SHORES, etc. etc. Why named after him? No particular reason, I gathered, except that it was good PR. Tourist stuff, I told myself, but it didn't keep me from setting off down the path.

The terrain was sandy, densely vegetated, bristling with cacti, lush with a profusion of West Indian plants, thick with the shade of buttonwood, false mastic and wild coffee trees. A "hammock" they called it in these Southern climes.

Stillness engulfed me. An intense quiet. A dim, leafy greenness. Fixed, spellbound, like a place that has not been disturbed for a thousand years. I was cut off from the road, from the rest of the Refuge, from all human congress. Swallowed up as though by some forest in an Arthurian legend.

All down the trail, idyllic sylvan images succeeded one another; an occasional thin shaft of sunlight filtering through branches to dapple the pale pink and gray of a tree trunk, a basketwork of thick gnarled roots partly submerged in a pool of copper-colored water, a flash of white among bottle-green leaves as an egret appeared and disappeared without a sound.

I fished in my shoulder bag for the binoculars and searched the surrounding branches for any other winged creature that might be sneaking around, but found none and walked on, stopping occasionally at one of the small signs that offered information about the exotic species of plant or tree growing in that spot. One of these signs announced that I was looking at the site of an old Indian mound. The nomadic Calusa Indians, as I knew from reading my history, had settled in these parts a good few thousand years ago, and built their villages on mounds composed of mollusk shells. I looked around. The ground was certainly covered with broken shells, but then so was a great deal of the island. Why this particular spot? It not only wasn't a mound, it was flatter than anything I'd passed so far: a rather uninteresting patch, relatively free of plant life, extending a hundred yards or so back from the path. Perhaps the mound was farther in, where the vegetation began. I looked through the glasses. No mound that I could see.

Then something red caught my eye. I fiddled with the focus, trying to get a closer look. I'd found some magnificent bird, if only I could make it out. Leaves and branches got in the way and I shifted my position, then lost it entirely. Patiently I moved the glasses in a slow arc along that section of greenery, found the red again, a small triangle, but couldn't distinguish head or beak or wing. If the silly thing would only *move*. I picked up a handful of broken shells, flung it as far as I could in the direction of the red blob, and quickly put the glasses back to my eyes. The shells fell on other shells with a tiny scatter of sound, but no glorious red bird took wing. Stubbornly the small triangle stayed where it was. I gave up and continued along the path.

I came upon a gumbo-limbo, towering beside the path, or so the sign said. It didn't look very much like the huge naked specimen near Sarah's home in Captiva. Sarah. By now she was surely working away with trowel and fertilizer at the Conservation Center, squatting on the ground, hair in her eyes, absently wiping her soiled fingers on her jeans, splashing a little weed killer on her red T-shirt . . .

I found myself staring at a strangler fig without seeing it, turned and walked back along the path to the Indian mound, put the glasses to my eyes. The red triangle was still there. Would a bird sit in the same position for so long? Why hadn't it been startled into flight by that scatter of shells? In this profound quiet, surely a sudden sharp sound, even a small one, would send any normal bird skyward.

Was it a plant? There was nothing that color anywhere else along the trail. It was too solid for a plant, too all of a piece. Nothing about it looked like a leaf or a flower, a stem or a stamen, a pod or a needle. It was just a red . . . something.

I could probably get closer to it by walking across that hundred yards of broken shells. I looked at the patch of ground: it looked firm enough, but who knew? I could find myself sinking ankledeep into some nameless ooze, and I had nothing on my feet but a pair of skimpy flat sandals. Besides, I simply must not become a slave to a foolish uneasiness, based on nothing but my mother's dredging up of an old movie plot. Sarah was at work, that's where she was. Period.

Thinking determinedly about lunch, I walked back along the trail to the point where I'd entered it, and over to where the car was parked. A pale-blue Dodge came down the road toward me, stopped, and a most surprising trio emerged from it: Grafman, Webber *and Ruskin*. Together at last. Had Ruskin and Grafman made up? Shaken hands, sent Alvin Persky on his way and decided to celebrate by coming to look at the birds?

"Your mother said to look for you here," Ruskin drawled.

My God, she'd fallen down! "What happened! Did she hurt herself?"

"This has nothing to do with your mother," Grafman growled, nervously tucking his unbuttoned pink chambray shirt into his maroon slacks. "We were looking for you."

"They want to ask you some questions," Ruskin interrupted, "didn't know how to get hold of you, came tearing up to my apartment—"

"I left my phone number for Thea," I said. "Didn't she—"

"I called your mother," Ruskin went on. "You told me she was bedridden, so I called on the phone instead of knocking at at the door. Considerate?"

Grafman spoke to some point over my shoulder, "I want to know—"

"We lost the note," Webber put in, looking as though he'd

chewed up all his nails and urgently needed a substitute, "with your phone number—"

"What"—Grafman's abrasive voice prevailed—"did Thea say to you yesterday?"

"She hasn't come back." Ruskin dropped the bomb and turned away to admire the scenery.

"Thea—?" I began.

"We haven't heard from her," Webber blurted.

"What," Grafman shouted, "did she say yesterday?"

"Say?" I tried to absorb the fact that Thea was still missing. What did it mean? Leroy? Sarah? "She—nothing, really. She was upset about the car being locked—"

"Did she say anything about where she was going when she was through here? You have any idea where she might have gone? You have any idea what was on her mind?" Grafman spoke impatiently, as though Thea's disappearance were something he'd rather not think about.

I found myself wishing I knew less about Thea. Or more. I couldn't even be certain that Sarah's information was fact and not conjecture. If Thea's connection with Leroy was innocent, how could I justify passing on a potentially damaging surmise? And if it was anything *but* innocent, I had no right at all to interfere. But twenty-four hours was a serious length of time for unexplained absence—

"Well?" Grafman tugged distractedly at his beard.

"I'm trying to think—" I struggled to remember if she'd given the slightest clue, closed my eyes and saw her standing beside the car, the fingers of one hand clutching her shirt, insisting she hadn't locked the door, wiping the sweat from her forehead, going unsteadily up the road in her tomato-colored shorts. . . .

"I'm sorry. She didn't say anything that could—I think she wasn't feeling well."

"Did she tell you that?"

"No, but she looked unwell. Maybe it was the heat. She might have . . . she was walking in this direction from the observation tower. This is just about the end of the Refuge road. If she didn't leave the Refuge—"

"Didn't *leave*?"

"—then this last stretch, between the tower and the exit, farther on, is the only place she could have gone."

They all began speaking at once.

"Have you notified the police?" I asked.

To a man, they ignored the question. Images chased one another past my inner eye. A small red triangle in the undergrowth. Sarah tapping her fingers against her camera. Leroy muscleproud behind the wheel of the same blue Dodge that now stood just beyond my mother's Ford. The possibilities multiplied, all of them distressing. There was only one way to settle it, and I believed, when faced with a choice of knowing or not knowing, that while either could be torment, *not* knowing lasted longer. Whoever, or whatever, that red triangle was part of, I had to know.

"Listen!" I said, cutting into their mutually obliterating gabble, "this is a chance in a hundred million, but I saw something—in there—"

Three heads turned to look at the entrance to the Gasparilla trail and stared at it as though expecting the emergence of some large South Florida reptile.

"Saw what?" Grafman asked, carefully.

"I'll show you."

They trooped down the trail after me, Grafman muttering that this was a waste of time, Ruskin ostentatiously looking bored, Webber mopping his brow, in spite of the cool shade through which we walked. When we reached the Indian mound I took out the glasses, and located the red triangle. They took turns at the glasses.

"So there's a piece of red something out there," Grafman rasped. "What are you showing me?"

"She was wearing red shorts," I said.

"Crap." Grafman shook his head in disgust.

Ruskin passed the glasses to Webber. "You know how many red things there are in heaven and earth, Horatio? Handkerchiefs, kites, paper napkins, kids' socks, balloons—"

T-shirts, I thought, not knowing any longer which girl I was afraid of finding.

"This is a waste of time," Grafman repeated.

"Why would she go out there?" Webber thrust the glasses back at me. "It's full of—who knows?—poison ivy, snakes—"

."If she wasn't feeling well," I argued, "and thought she was going to be sick, and didn't want to . . . mess up the trail . . ."

"I've been sick in my day," Ruskin said through his nose, "and believe me, no sick person is going to wander into a swamp full of alligators just to keep things tidy."

"It doesn't look like a swamp."

"For Christ's sake"—Grafman lit a cigarillo—"this is getting us nowhere. If she went to find somebody to unlock the car, why would she come in here? Let's go." He started back up the trail.

"It wouldn't hurt," I said firmly, "for someone to go out and take a closer look."

"Be my guest—" He kept going, and Ruskin and Webber turned to follow.

Some attitudes provoke me to foolish retaliation. Clenching my jaw, I stepped off the road and took three determined strides across the broken shells.

"Hey!" Webber yelled.

Ruskin grabbed my arm. "Be a nice grown-up person and come out of there."

Grafman came back, scowling. "Women," he muttered.

"I haven't heard *that* one," I said, "since nineteen-sixty," and shaking off Ruskin's hand, I kept going, outwardly fearless, inwardly trembling, scanning the ground ahead of me, stepping carefully around anonymous green tufts and spears, praying the earth beneath my sandals would stay dry and solid. Behind me I heard the reluctant scrunching of three pairs of feet, following.

A few yards from the beginning of the underbrush I stopped and looked toward where the red triangle should be, saw it, and turned away, suddenly faint and icy cold.

CHAPTER TEN

THERE WAS FOG ON THE BEACH EARLY THE NEXT MORNing. Sand, water and sky were wrapped in a grayish gauze, the beach deserted, a silence so complete that the cry of a gull barely pricked it. I walked along the hard-packed sand at the edge of the Gulf, alone in a foggy, gull-specked world. Gray mist, gray Gulf, white sand, and the gray-and-white gulls scattered about. A Nantucket scene.

And in the midst of all this scrupulous gray and white, one black bird sitting among the gulls, stretching its neck to utter a hoarse cry, as though trying to dislodge a bone stuck in its throat. A crow? I was in no mood for ornithology.

But how that one scrap of black stood out from everything around it. Easy enough, I thought, to spot the aberrant bird when it's a different color from all the rest. How do you pick it out, though, when the flock it's sitting among is a motley collection of shapes and sizes and irregularities, each bird as odd as the next? Impossible to identify the anomaly then, the dangerously different bird, the killer bird.

There'd been a killing, that was certain. They might mumble about "accidents," but they didn't really believe it. No one knew what Thea had died of, but natural causes seemed highly unlikely. Ruskin, of course, had been right: alone and taken ill, the human animal doesn't make for some isolated and unpredictable piece of ground. She would have gone toward people, toward help, not away from it. No, she'd been put there, *hidden* there.

And I had found her. Worrying about a Sarah dangerously bent on ridding herself of a threat, I'd found the woman who was a threat to her.

"What made you think that little bit of red color you saw in the bushes could be Miss Quinn?" The investigative sergeant had been properly polite, impersonal.

"She'd been wearing that color. Red shorts. And—uh—the last time I saw her she was walking in that direction. And . . . she was missing . . . so . . . ."

We'd gone into my impression that she hadn't been feeling well: What made you think so? Was she short of breath? Pain in her chest? No, just seemed very hot, possibly nauseated, disoriented, yes, maybe dizzy, she didn't say. They asked Grafman if she had any history of heart trouble. "She was twenty-six!" he barked. "She could swim a mile and not feel it! She could stay out all night and look like a goddam *rose* in the morning! She grew up on a *ranch,* for Christ's sake! Why don't you ask the guy who's going to open her up? He'll see for himself!"

Was she on any medications? Did she use drugs? "Not even aspirin!"

It was Webber who volunteered that she was an antidrug crusader. She'd known someone, he said, who had turned into a vegetable, and she was terrified of drugs.

"I can see the way your mind works!" Grafman's face, bloodless under the tan, looked gray. "Show business! Cocaine! We're *working* here, goddam it! This isn't some freaked-out beach party! This is dollars and cents!"

Had she been depressed? Was there any reason she might have—?

"She was *Catholic*! She was very, very Catholic! You understand?"

There'd been no visible clue, she was unmarked. "Lucky," I heard an officer mumble, "she was hidden under those trees, the buzzards didn't spot her."

Thea had been taken to the county morgue. Golden Thea, radiant Thea. The young officer with the new moustache had arrived in his brown-and-tan police car, "secured the scene," spoken to the dispatcher on his police radio about notifying the Chief and the Refuge manager and the emergency services, and they'd taken her away. And then we sat answering questions in the bright, clean offices of police headquarters on the second floor of the pale-green building on the San–Cap road, with the City Council Chamber beneath us and a gas station between us and the road.

Ruskin's face had gone blank and his tongue speechless. Webber was a death's-head. I had kept my eyes on the captain of police. Big, solid, weathered, in a smart tan uniform with two gold bars on each shoulder, the letters SPD sitting with casual authority on collar and sleeves, and a face that had no use for pomp or self-importance; a relaxed, interested, not-for-sale face. In the heaving sea on which I was tossing he'd seemed a likely rock to cling to, and if he had been the one to question me I might have said more. As it was, I hadn't.

Having slept minimally since then, I felt both restless and exhausted. My throat was scratchy. That may have been the red tide doing its well-known job of irritating the respiratory tract, but more probably it was a reaction to yesterday's horror and the rumblings of my conscience. Psychosoma was an old enemy. I trudged on, wondering how much farther the lighthouse could be. My mother had called it "a good long walk," but it had already been a long one and the beach seemed to stretch ahead of me to infinity in an unbroken sameness. No promontory or peninsula was visible on which a lighthouse might reasonably be expected to sit. Still, it must be there somewhere, and what else was there to do?

There *was* something, of course, but I wasn't prepared to do it, and that, as much as anything, was making me feel less than well. I'd been questioned by police and I hadn't told what I knew: more accurately, I told myself, coming up with instant justification, the one thing I knew and others I'd only heard about. Yes, Sarah had said she was going to use her camera to cause trouble between Thea and "the man who paid the bills," but people were always threatening unlikely things in a fit of frustration, "So help me I'll kill him" not to be taken literally.

It was not a *fact* that she was going to do it. The only *fact* I possessed was that I'd seen Thea with a young man.

That his name was Leroy, that he worked at the marina, that Thea was carrying on some *sub rosa* romance with him, that Grafman was planning to build a house for Thea on the tract of land next to Sarah McChesney, that Sarah was violently opposed to this and planning to forestall the purchase of the property by the use of blackmail—all of that was secondhand information and surmise. All that I knew for certain was that Thea had been visiting that plot of land with a muscular young man, five eleven or thereabouts, with dark hair and a toothy smile.

Suppose, I argued mentally, that I gave the police that one piece of information, told them I'd seen Thea with that man, what could they do with it? They would have to postulate the possibility of a sexual relationship and that would raise the question of jealousy on Grafman's part. They'd question Grafman, and if he said he knew the man, his name was Leroy, and so on, the police would have one more piece of information. But Grafman would have to be pretty dim to admit to any knowledge that might make him a prime suspect. He'd say he knew nothing about any such man, and the police would have gained nothing from my telling them, strictly and solely, what I'd *seen:* they still wouldn't know the man's identity. For that, I'd have to tell them what I'd *heard* as well.

And, of course, telling the police anything at all at this late date would be tricky.

"Why didn't you mention this yesterday?"

Because, Sergeant, for some intuitive and probably ill-advised reason, I'm protecting someone. Hardly.

Why, then? I forgot? I was too upset? The police were no fools, and the questions wouldn't end there. What was I doing on the tract of land? Asking about a tree? Asking whom? What young woman? What's her name? Did she see the young man? Did she know him?

Talk about a can of worms . . .

I had reached what appeared to be the end of the beach, and still no lighthouse. Vegetation grew almost to the water's edge and I could see nothing beyond it. But there must be more. Walking on a narrow strip of sand and rocks, I rounded the screen of trees and bushes, and saw, just ahead, two identical and immaculate white frame one-story buildings that stood well off the ground on iron stilts.

Just beyond them rose a hundred-foot-high cylinder supported and surrounded by an iron framework and topped by an octagonal glass room: the Sanibel Light. Almost a century old, I'd read in my *History,* fed first on kerosene and then acetylene gas, the keepers climbing up and down its spiral staircase to keep it burning through storms and hurricanes and the darkness of three wars.

I walked up to the two white buildings that backed into the beach. They both looked roomy, bright, and in excellent repair. Not to mention the view. I couldn't recall, in any of the gothic literature that had peppered my adolescence, that lighthouse keepers ever lived this well. Cobwebs and must and gloomy lanterns amid the crashing seas were their lot.

For that matter, the light itself was out of character. Where was the classic tower of dark and ancient brick? This, frankly, looked more like something out of White Sands, New Mexico. Inside the iron framework that surrounded it, an enclosure of wire mesh topped with barbed wire protected the ladder that stretched fifteen feet up to a landing outside the padlocked door that, in turn, opened into the cistern. Once inside the cistern, I supposed, a spiral staircase led to the top. Or, if that last romantic vestige had also vanished, then ye olde lighthouse keeper ascended in some kind of hydraulic lift, the sooner to get the chores over with and back to the latest episode of *Dallas* on the box.

Next to the Sanibel Light stood the only structure that spoke of times past: a white-painted brick shed about six feet high with an ancient paneled wooden door of faded gray. A sign on the wall proclaimed that this was the oil house, built in 1884.

I gazed for a while at the small square brick house to which, a hundred years ago, men had come in the dead of night for the grease-blackened canisters of oil they carried through the lashing rain to feed the light that saved the ships. Lost in a fantasy of masts keeling over in heavy weather, decks under water, ships' officers clinging to the bridge shouting "All hands on deck!" I heard, incredibly, the urgent clang of a ship's bell.

I looked up, startled. Had the delicate balance of my mind been disturbed? Was I bonkers?

No, there was a bell. It came from the road beyond the intervening trees, and it belonged to the cheerful red trolley that carried the car-less around and about the island to see the sights, do their shopping, or go to the beach. As period as a prop from *Meet Me in St. Louis,* with shiny wooden slatted benches and frosted patterns on the glass of its doors and fanlight windows, it tootled along the length of Periwinkle Way and the Gulf drives, ringing its bell at each stop to alert potential customers.

There were no customers waiting for it at the lighthouse stop this early in the day, but it had apparently picked up a few on its way here and they alighted from it now: an elderly couple, a less elderly couple, and two young women. Sightseeing. Carefree.

I wondered what Grafman and company were doing this morning. It must be hell sitting around The Gulls. In that apartment. With her clothes hanging in the closet, her scent on the sofa cushions. And no work to do, now. I thought of Persky, working away the day before, while the rest of us were walking down the Gasparilla trail. Sitting there inventing scenes for a leading lady who was past all performing. Turning my back to the sightseeing group, I made my way around the nearer of the two white houses and on to the beach. There were people walking along the water's edge now. Shelling, of course. I saw a sand collar, beached, and put it back in the shallow water with a piece of driftwood to anchor it, as Sarah had done.

Sarah.

She was alive, that much I knew. I'd confirmed that. It was the first thing I'd done when I got back from headquarters. Sick, shaken, so wrung out my mother's face blanched at sight of me, I made straight for the phone and dialed that number. And Sarah had answered. Unmistakably Sarah's voice.

"Yes? Hello! Who is this? Answer me!"

"Sorry," I mumbled, "wrong number," while relief flooded me.

Sarah.

Could a girl who worried about sand-collar eggs being allowed to hatch possibly be guilty of taking a human life? The idea was appalling, but I couldn't sidestep the question. Because if there had been a confrontation between Sarah on the one hand and Thea and Leroy on the other, any violence would have left Sarah the victim, not Thea. As it was, if there *had* been a confrontation (no Leroy, no picture to take, Sarah frustrated, desperate), then it would only have been between the two women alone. And Thea was dead. And where had Sarah been that night? And the following morning?

Oh don't be an ass, I told myself. How do you know she doesn't have a man somewhere to spend the night with? Why must you put the most lurid interpretation on every incident?

Because, damn it, the last time I saw her she had fire in her eye and a camera in her hand and Thea's downfall was her stated purpose.

Well then, hand her over to the police. Let them tackle it and let Sarah take care of herself.

Oh yes, that's a picture. Sarah standing up to the police. Reticent Sarah, who tells a virtual stranger she's planning to compromise someone with her camera. One question from the police and the floodgates would open, washing her downstream and right into the tightly woven net from which suspects emerge—if they do—considerably more familiar with neurosis than they had previously been. In Sarah's case, with her awesome talent for self-incrimination, possibly into a cell.

Which, possibly, is where she belongs.

But possibly not.

It could be Grafman. It could be Leroy. It could be person or persons unknown. Some psychopath, set adrift from the mainland to float up onto this tranquil island shore. . . .

The fog, I noticed without much interest, had been dispersed, and a white disk of sun was baking the beach. I trudged heavily homeward. My pace had slowed to that of an infirm snail. My limbs seemed to be made of concrete. Tired was not the word to describe my condition. There *was* no word. I'd been weary before in my life, God knows. Carrying three suitcases through the taxiless streets of Paris to the Gare du Nord on a thirty-first of July had left me memorably fatigued. Trundling forty-six loads of autumn leaves in a wheelbarrow from copse to curb in an effort to speed the arrival of an overdue baby had resulted in epic exhaustion. But the burdens I had carried then paled beside the weight I seemed to have been supporting for the last twenty-four hours. Atlas, I decided, had had it easy. Indecision was a lot heavier than the pillars of heaven.

At long last I reached the stretch of sand adjoining the Sea Grape grounds, and sank with an audible groan into an unoccupied deck chair. Only then, relieved of the responsibility of keeping myself upright, did I allow myself a shred of optimism. There was one tiny, frail hope, that in addition to the alternatives of telling the police or not telling the police, one other course of action might be open to me. I'd baited a trap, the night before. Whether or not it had been sprung remained to be seen. I prayed, in my atheistic fashion, that it had. My face lifted to the sun, I closed my eyes.

When I opened them again, the skin of my face felt unusually taut. God, how long had I been asleep? And no sun guard on my nose! I consulted my wrist: the watch was upstairs on the dresser. What time was it? I hadn't prepared lunch for the patient! She probably thought I'd walked all the way to Fort Myers looking for the lighthouse.

I untangled myself from the deck chair and stumbled over the sand toward the Sea Grape, no longer tired but with that fidgety disorientation that comes from sleeping when all about you are at work or play. Climbed the outside staircase to the apartment feeling gritty and hollow. I'd had nothing but an orange for breakfast, perhaps that was it: hunger. I could have used a little food for the spirit, that was certain. A few shimmering passages of Ravel or Debussy. Some soothing pastoral Delius would have been nice, too. And a calm, orderly helping of Telemann. I listened for a sound from Ruskin's apartment. I would have settled for the Minute Waltz. There was nothing.

I unlocked the door. There was a suitcase standing in the middle of the living room floor.

I looked at it, touched it to make sure it was really there. That same suitcase had made a trip to the Berkshires in the trunk of my car only days before a violinist had died onstage during an orchestra rehearsal. It had accompanied my own case on a plane south and a train north, in pursuit of evidence against a Sloan's Ford criminal. It was a suitcase that belonged on the third floor of a white house on Poplar Avenue. The trap had been sprung.

I strode down the hallway. By some superhuman effort my mother had maneuvered herself into a pair of lavender slacks and a fresh white shirt, and was furiously brushing her hair.

"He might have let us know he was coming!" she fumed. "I look like a piece of seaweed!"

"Where is he?"

She gestured toward the window with the brush. "Hanging out," she said in her fluty Elizabethan voice, "down there."

I went the window and looked out. Down below, standing by the pool regarding the alien sybaritic surroundings with the fortitude of a vegetarian trapped in a steakhouse, was the long, pensive figure of Charles Benjamin Greenfield: crumpled chinos, plaid shirt, wispy gray hair and all.

CHAPTER ELEVEN

"**C**HARLIE" I CRIED, ALL SWEET SURPRISE. "HOW come?"

He turned from his contemplation of the sunbathers around the pool, gave me a long, cautionary look, and spoke in a muted voice with great deliberation. "Dissembling," he said, "is the least you can spare me. You *arranged* this."

"Arranged what?"

He stared at the ground, then at a palmetto. Finally, "I've had a trying day. I've spent three and a half hours removed by some thirty thousand feet from the solid ground on which man was meant to stand. On several occasions only the intervention of an unaccountable thermodynamic benevolence prevented that machine, with me in it, from ending up a crumpled, blackened mass on some mountaintop. Don't," he added very softly, "horse around." He moved away from me toward the path that led to the beach.

"Well, I'm delighted to see you. I'm just sur—"

"You called me"—prowling down the path, he measured out the words a teaspoon at a time—"and said you couldn't leave this island"—pushed aside a protruding branch—"until

80

you knew your mother was safe from a possible psychopath who is at large here"—stepped aside to avoid a running child—"and who has murdered some woman in a nature preserve." We emerged on the beach. "It's been known to take months—years—for the police to apprehend the correct psychopath. I don't have years. To judge by my present condition I may not even have days. In the meantime, for better or worse, putting out a newspaper is what I do, and I can't do it without staff. As you were well aware when you made that call."

"So that's why you're here. To take me back by brute force."

He stopped at the edge of the beach and turned to face me. "If there were any justice, you'd be charged with two crimes. One, you're holding yourself for ransom. That's kidnapping."

"Oh come, now—"

"And two, you've extorted my presence here by means of a threat. That's blackmail."

"Black—!" His eyes warned me not to go on. "All right, maybe blackmail," I admitted. "It's possible I caught it. There's a lot of it going around."

He nodded grimly, and having established the basis on which we were to proceed, namely, that he was here but he wasn't going to like it, he stood, hands deep in his pockets, and stared out across the sand from under the straggling gray vegetation known as his eyebrows. In quiet, implacable disgruntlement he regarded the Gulf of Mexico and found it wanting. He scanned the beach; no desk, no creaking swivel chair, no outlet for a stereo, the beach was a dead loss.

"Think of it as a change of pace," I said, "a long weekend. The *Reporter* went to press last night. Stewart can supervise the delivery. If Calli's got the flu she'll be useless for another week anyway, and if Helen's come down with it, Spartan though she is, she won't be in until Tuesday at the earliest. The twenty-second is coming up, you could run a repeat of the historical issue—"

(I'd heard that story often enough. Some years before I'd come on the scene, Greenfield's small staff, in an excess of office camaraderie, had all gone off on a skiing weekend and been stranded upstate by a blizzard. Greenfield, forced to throw his integrity to the winds, had pounced on George Washington's upcoming birthday and put out a paper consisting solely of an account of Washington's sojourn, at the time of the battle of White Plains, in the area that later became Sloan's Ford. He fleshed it out with images of the army sneaking past enemy outposts in the dead of night, headlined it *Washington Crept Here*, then struck the headline, settled for subtlety and quoted Washington's "Harmony and a liberal intercourse with all nations are recommended by policy, humanity and interest.")

"You could call Stewart and tell him to dig it up," I said.

No comment. He walked out onto the hot beach in his suede loafers.

I suggested he take off his shoes and socks so as not to get them full of sand. My solicitude fell on deaf ears. He continued down toward the water, giving no quarter.

I caught up with him. "This is not irresponsible behavior on my part, Charlie, not a whim. I have a serious ethical problem. I couldn't leave here without resolving it. I needed help. I needed a second opinion."

Finally he spoke. "I don't know how you do it."

"Do what?"

Would he give me a simple answer? Not while the earth revolved around the sun.

"How many people from various parts of the country," he asked, "would you say are currently visiting the island?"

"I don't know. Fifteen thousand. Or so."

"People from Vermont, Illinois, Wisconsin, South Dakota—"

"I wouldn't be surprised."

"New Jersey, Idaho, the Carolinas—"

"Could be."

"Utah, Nebraska—"

"*So?*"

"And yet," he went on doggedly, "with a cross section of the entire national population available for the purpose, it was *you* who had to be the last known person to see the murdered woman alive. And *you* who had to discover the body." He was briefly silent, contemplating my talent for prevailing against the odds. "How did you manage to overlook being apprehended with the murder weapon in your hand?"

"There was no weapon."

"If it was murder, there was a weapon. A piece of string is a weapon. A venomous snake is a weapon. A limb from a tree is a weapon."

"I can just see myself wielding a venomous snake."

"No doubt you'll manage that," he murmured, "on your next trip."

I forgave him. He had a right to be touchy. I followed as he trudged along the shore. "Charlie, the fact is, it's a sticky situation." Carefully I brought out the big gun, "There's a lot more to it than the police are aware of."

I expected that to stop him in his tracks, but it didn't. "Keeping things from the police," he said, "is a minor offense compared to ending a sentence with a preposition."

Oh, now, wait a minute. Touchy is understandable, but surly is something else! I fought the urge to retaliate. "Do you want to hear about it?"

"I didn't come for the scenery." He took possession of an unoccupied beach chair, dragging it farther away from the line of dead fish.

"Shall I give it to you in detail?"

"How many details are there?"

"Several hundred."

"Economy was never your strong point."

No, and civility is slipping fast. "Details, then. You'll have to know them sooner or later."

He dug the back legs of the chair into the sand until it tilted slightly backward and sat, long legs stretched out and crossed at the ankles. The chair didn't whine or swivel, but it was as close as he could get. I dropped onto the sand beside his chair while he gazed dully at a sandpiper skittering along the shore, and began with my first sight of Ruskin and Webber on the beach.

He listened to my account with an abstracted, apathetic air that was uncharacteristic and worrisome. Ordinarily his hackles would rise at the thought of a killer at large, his long face would go still with resolve, or at the very least his gaze would sharpen. But now he sat slack-limbed and indifferent, and the light of battle was conspicuously absent from his eyes. It was as unsettling as seeing Hamlet listen to his father's tale and yawn. Toward the end I wondered if he'd even been listening. I tested him.

"—and when we'd finished sitting around the police station answering questions," I went on, "Grafman said 'But that is the beginning of a new story, the story of the gradual renewal of a man, the story of his gradual regeneration—' "

"Did he say it in Russian?" Greenfield asked dryly.

He'd been listening, all right.

"Go on," he said.

"That's it. The police said we could go, they'd appreciate our being available for further questions if necessary, and we left. That's all, except that I didn't tell them what I knew. And I was hoping I wouldn't have to."

Greenfield got up without offering any comment, wandered down to the tidemark, and looked out at the Gulf, looked at it with an effort, like a child with a bellyache looking at a bowl of soup.

How long, O Lord, was this going to go on? All right, I'd conned him, but he'd had his fun with that, he'd made his point, no need to beat a dead issue. It was half playacting anyway, had to be, because if he was honest with himself (and that he usually was, though not always with everyone else), he had to admit that in the past he had finagled *me,* time and again, into what he called "tracking down a humanoid." Finagled me, what's more, into situations that gave me nothing but cold sweats and headaches while they gave him an opportunity to exercise his brain and his flair. Morality aside, for him they were the next best thing to fighting his way through a Mozart trio to the last satifying chord. Why, then, was he behaving as though he were bloody *bored*?

Well, there was one thing that might jolt him back to life.

I walked down to where he stood with the water lapping at the sand an inch from his shoes. A small pink-fleshed woman had engaged him in conversation. She had a bird's nest of white hair, wore long black knit shorts reminiscent of a Mack Sennett bathing beauty, and gestured with the clamming shovel she held in one hand.

"It's the red tide," she piped. "It kills the fish and they get washed up here. Paralyzes them, some poison that's in the Gulf, a poisonous plant that grows out there, under the water. You'd think they'd clean up the beach, after all, people come here for vacation, it's not right that the beach should be full of dead fish. But I suppose they can't afford to hire people to do it. Who can afford anything these days, I'd like to know. This shovel—it's for clams, you know, but I don't clam in the red tide, I'm just digging up shells—you know what this shovel cost me? Last year—just last year, mind you, I paid, let's see, two-fifty for one of these. Two-fifty-five, I remember exactly. Know what they're asking now? Four-ninety-eight. Five dollars! For a piece of tin. Now, if that's not inflation I'd like to know what is. And they keep telling us the economy's getting better. What's economical about five dollars for a shovel, I'd like to know!''

I rescued him. We walked back over the sand toward the Sea Grape.

''I need a place to stay,'' he said.

''There's plenty of room. Two beds in my mother's room. I'll just move my things.''

''I have no intention—''

''Charlie, it's not that kind of place.'' I swept an arm down the beach. ''Whatever isn't an apartment is a condominium. No rentals by the day.''

''There is no place in America that doesn't have at least one aesthetically barbarous motel.''

''If there is a motel, they won't have anything available, it's the height of the season. Besides,'' I lied, ''my mother wouldn't hear of any other arrangement.''

Ordinarily he would have gone on arguing for another ten minutes; today, apparently it wasn't worth the trouble.

I pointed to the end of the parking lot. ''That yellow Ford, Charlie. Wait there, I'll get the keys. We have an hour to sundown, we're going to the Refuge.''

Driving down Periwinkle and up the San-Cap road, I chatted briskly, pointing out the bookstore, the shopping center where Thea had been photographed near the fountain, the police station, the Conservation Center. Inside the Refuge I showed him where Thea's car had been parked next to the observation tower, and finally, the spot where I'd first caught sight, through the binoculars, of that significant patch of red.

Across the front of the Indian mound a strip of bright-yellow three-inch plastic tape was stretched between stakes driven into the ground. Printed on the bright-yellow background, stern black letters broadcast a warning: POLICE LINE DO NOT CROSS.

An officer in brown and tan patrolled quietly, and a few straggling sightseers were sidling by the site, casting a wary eye at it, but otherwise the scene was as otherworldly as I remembered it.

Greenfield stood in the hushed, dappled depths of the Gasparilla trail and stared past the stretch of crushed shell to the distant clumps of underbrush that had hidden Thea.

"This is not," he observed, "the crossroads of the world."

"Exactly."

"She wasn't dim enough to come here looking for someone to unlock her car."

"Right again."

"And she was hardly in the right frame of mind for sightseeing."

Good, I thought. A spark of interest.

The patrolman was watching us, but he was out of earshot.

"If she was ambulatory when she reached this point," Greenfield mused halfheartedly, "then she was enticed out there. If not, she was carried." He treated the expanse of shell to a desultory scouting. "One person carrying another person generally makes an impression on the terrain. Of course"—with a glance at the officer—"a virtual army has marched over it since then. The time to notice if the shell had been disturbed was when you first saw it. I don't suppose you remember."

I stared at the haphazard scattering. "Who knows how it's supposed to look when it's *not* disturbed?"

He nodded and ambled back up the trail. The spark had gone out.

"Where do you think we should start?" I prodded.

"This is your operation. Don't you have a program in mind?"

Since when do I determine programs, Charlie? That's your province. I'm a legperson: point me and I go.

"I could make up a reference sheet," I said, "a list of the people involved, with the pertinent information."

"That's a nice clerical procedure. Then what?"

It was at this point that spontaneous combustion occurred.

"I don't *know* then what! Then *everything!* One thing leads to another! Mostly you trot out some of that vaunted mental agility of yours!''

He stopped beside the sign at the entrance to the trail, and stared at me thoughtfully for a while. Now I've wakened him up, I thought. I should have done that an hour ago. He sighed. He spoke.

''Make up the reference sheet,'' he said, and went to the car and got in.

Oh, sparkling. Oh my, such cerebral fireworks. For the first time I wondered if his apathy could be so deeply entrenched that nothing I could do would dissipate it. You can lead a man to a problem but you can't, after all, make him think. With a dreadful feeling of futility I got behind the wheel.

''Charlie,'' I said quietly, ''are you coming down with the flu? Is the *Reporter* going bankrupt? Is anything wrong with Julie, or Karen, or Debbie, or the grandkids?''

''No,'' he said, ''and no, and no.''

''Or—um—anybody else?'' A useful, all-inclusive question that could encompass not only his widely scattered friends but the woman about whom we had all speculated from time to time over the years, whenever there was an unexplained phone call at the office or a mysterious batch of brownies on his desk that came from no bakery, and certainly not from the oven of any of his three daughters, devoted as their kitchens were to carrot juice, sashimi, zucchini bread and the like. He'd been a widower for twelve years, a celibate at the most, I suspected, for one. ''Everybody's okay?''

''Everybody,'' he said flatly, ''is fine.''

''Then, please, if you don't mind, for God's sake, for my sanity, tell me what country you're in and when you're coming back.''

There was a long silence. In that silence the opening scene of *Troilus and Cressida* could have been written. The first movement of the ''Waldstein'' could have been composed. Michelangelo could have painted the Almighty's entire creating hand, index finger and all. Greenfield sat with his elbow where the window glass would have been if the window hadn't been open, eyes fixed on some point beyond the windshield, chin pushed up into his lower lip.

Finally he said, ''I find it difficult to worry about apprehending one psychopath among so many in this world. The earth is crawling with them. Moscow and Washington are overrun with psychopaths masquerading as statesmen, government officials, public servants. They inhabit London, Beirut, Johannesburg, La Paz, they cover the globe. It's become a commonplace to say that the thugs have taken over, and the mere repetition of the phrase drains it of meaning, as Mr. Bellow pointed out. 'There are evils that survive identification.' The psychopaths, identified, are running things. The rest of us are irrelevant. Civilization is irrelevant. Wisdom is irrelevant. The psychopath is in control; the terrorist in the bushes, the gunrunner in the alley, the board chairman of the chemical plant, above all, the genius with the charts and figures to prove that destroying life on earth will not interfere with business as usual.''

He turned his head to the window and propped it up with the hand that happened to be there. ''In the face of that, the prospect of tracking down one relatively modest murderer can hardly be expected to make my adrenaline flow.''

I sat there, speechless, while the sun sank into tangerine clouds that slowly turned to violet, and finally disappeared, and Greenfield asked, plaintively, if there was any possibility of dinner.

All the way back down the San–Cap road and Periwinkle, all during the time that Greenfield was in the Gourmet Take-Out purchasing Cornish game hens and a lemon mousse, and in the liquor store acquiring a bottle of Montrachet, I found it impossible to speak. Greenfield's abdication in the face of madness was worse than anything I might have predicted. I could think of no way to reverse it.

We climbed the outside stairway and I heard music issuing once again from Ruskin's apartment. Greenfield heard it too and paused, listening. I could see him wondering if, after all, there might be one saving grace to this enforced visit. Then he realized it was *The Sorcerer's Apprentice*. He looked at me. ''Is that typical of the collection?''

I nodded glumly. ''It's a kind of Child's Garden of Classical Music.''

His shoulders sagged and he continued up the stairs.

A lovely basket of fruit all done up in amber cellophane stood on the dining table: the coals Greenfield had brought from New York to Newcastle for the invalid. I unwrapped it, moved it to the coffee table, and in some kind of last-ditch effort, gave Greenfield my *History of the Islands*, open at the chapter on Gasparilla, to read while I warmed the food and prepared a salad. He had read the chapter and closed the book without comment by the time we sat down to eat.

Dinner was a strained affair, the lady of the house trying (while repeatedly darting troubled glances to left and to right, from my dejected face to Greenfield's remote expression and back again) to give the impression she was in command of a smoothly run establishment unfazed by drop-in guests. Halfway through the game hen she gave up and said, with her characteristic mixture of conflicting decorum and idiom, "This is no way to behave at table. Whatever one of you said to the other, apologize and let's get this show on the road." Whereupon Greenfield obliged with an informative discourse on the terrors of the fourteenth century as described in the Barbara Tuchman he'd brought to read on the plane.

Commenting on the killing, pillaging and general beastliness of the Hundred Years' War, the invalid observed that nothing had really changed. "Men are going to go on committing atrocities as long as they have reason to feel guilty."

Greenfield looked utterly lost.

"War," she explained patiently, "is popular because men feel a sense of guilt over how little they do in life compared with women. Women have always worked at least twice as many hours a day as men, they've always had a harder time of it, and men know it. Men *know* they've been getting a free ride, and going to war is the only way they can equalize things. They make up in danger and physical hardship what they've escaped in drudgery."

Mother had been at the barricades before the word "feminism" was coined. My father had sometimes agreed, sometimes argued, mostly been bewildered by the duality of her nature. Greenfield, after a judicious pause, took a deep breath and murmured, "Interesting."

Later, standing with eyes closed under the shower, letting the downpour beat on my neck and shoulders, I considered the problem of Greenfield's unprecedented surrender to the odds.

Yes, of course, this was a teapot tempest by comparison with global chaos and, yes, it was a temptation to take that route, to say, "Terrible that a young woman was killed, too bad if another young woman is implicated, but there you are, the world's a bloody disaster anyway," and sink into Stygian gloom. But in the end you couldn't choose desolation as a way of life. Certainly Charles Benjamin *Greenfield* never could. Never *had*.

He was, beyond everything else, a fighter. He had always fought every offense to a civilized and humanitarian way of life that came within his orbit, from the third-grade writing skills of high school graduates to the dumping of toxic materials on an undeveloped tract two miles outside the village, knowing that in the first instance it would take a miracle to resurrect the importance of the written word, and in the second that organized crime might find him enough of a nuisance to send out a man with a fly swatter. He had never before bothered with the odds.

Why now? Why suddenly give up? Retire, defeated? Sit glumly on the deck and go down with the ship, just another doomed passenger?

Then it struck me. He was *here*, wasn't he? He'd got himself into a taxi and out to the airport and onto a plane, and he was *here*. Why do all that if he believed there was no point to it? Why not ignore my implied threat, pull the blinds, put a Brandenburg on the stereo and wait for Armageddon?

He wasn't defeated. He wasn't broken. What he was, was mad as hell. He was so bloody angry he could barely move. The latest piece of towering idiocy, of criminally stupid international street fighting, had sent him beyond teeth-gnashing and acid commentary into dark, inexpressible, paralytic fury. Cosmic rage was what it was.

He was here. Probably because he couldn't resist being indispensable, and that was all to the good. He was here. In a state of bottomless depression and keening all the way, but here. To work.

It would just take a little longer to get him started, like a car in winter.

In the bedroom my mother bookmarked her Doris Lessing and shut it. "Do you understand this?" she demanded, brandishing the book.

"Sure," I said, "it's her way of giving up on *this* planet." I wrapped myself in my robe and went in search of Greenfield.

He sat on the balcony, gazing out at the dark, waving palms. The "Barcarolle" from *The Tales of Hoffman* trickled drowsily from Ruskin's apartment. There was no one on the Ruskin balcony, but who knew when there might be.

"Come inside," I said, and in the lamplit living room I appropriated a corner of the sofa, turned the key in Greenfield's ignition and stepped gently on the accelerator. "What did you think of the Gasparilla story?"

"As a hint," he said, "it had all the subtlety of a Von Suppé overture."

"As a parallel, it has even less. But these are not necessarily subtle people. These are theater people. They put a proscenium around everything."

"The most level-headed man I ever met was an actor. He went to work every day, collected his paycheck, and spent his time off doing carpentry and rearing five sensible children."

"All right, generalizing is tricky, but by and large they tend to see themselves center stage. Who's more of a pirate king than Grafman? And who was more of a princess than Thea? He was obsessed with her, Ruskin said so, and anyway, it was obvious. She may have slept in his bed, but he behaved as though he were still trying to get her there. Possessive, but apprehensive. She treated him with a kind of—teasing intimacy. The way a woman behaves who wants to keep a man enthralled but won't make a total commitment to him. In the meantime she takes up with Leroy. If Gasparilla found the princess playing with a lowly sailor, what would he have done? In fact, he *did* it, even though the princess wasn't playing, but only keeping him at arm's length. Rejection is rejection, whether it's direct or by implication."

"I gather you're postulating that this man Grafman is so devoid of imagination that he had to have someone else think up the plot before it occurred to him to commit murder."

"Listen. Isn't it possible Grafman decided to produce this show because he identified with Gasparilla? What if he was having trouble with Thea even then, when he first read the script? He saw Thea as the princess. He *cast* her as the princess. And he's been living with the story ever since, working on it day and night, chewing it over. Picture of a strong man wounded in his male pride by a noncompliant woman. That kind of thing can prey on your mind. It's there in front of him every day: *Gasparilla killed the princess!*"

Greenfield leaned back in the armchair with a handful of grapes from the fruit basket. "In that case," he said, "we have nothing to do. He'll wrap an anchor around himself and jump into the Gulf. Call the airline and book two seats."

"*Come* on, Charlie! *Try*."

He ate a grape. "You realize, I hope, that Archimedes, much as he wanted to illustrate the principle of the lever by moving the entire world, never did find the vantage point from which to do it. That Thomas Edison, persistent though he was, conducted endless experiments in an attempt to produce a substitute for rubber and failed." He took another grape. "That Napoleon tried desperately, after he'd taken Moscow, and couldn't get the Czar to sign a peace treaty." Greenfield was not one to place himself in plebeian company. "If trying," he went on, "were a guarantee of success, Sir Francis Younghusband would have reached the summit of Everest long before Hillary: he *tried* three times. Da Vinci—"

"Please," I cut in, "wherever this historical tour is going to end up, let's not take the scenic route. As the crow flies, if you don't mind."

"I mind, but I'm a guest here." He popped the last grape into his mouth. "Let's understand something: I have no desire to settle down on this island. I'll do what I can for a limited period of time. But bearing in mind that some of the most determined men in history have had an occasional failure, I want your assurance that if, by Monday, I still don't have an inkling, we will both be on that two-thirty plane."

I sat quietly, my mind racing. There were two significant words in what he'd said. The first, obviously, was "Monday." But the second was "inkling." To my mind an inkling, a hint, and a suspicion were all the same thing. It was a pretty good bet that by Monday he'd have, for God's sake, if not an actual suspicion, at least a *hint*.

"Done," I said. "Now. What about this Gasparilla legend?"

"If it's relevant at all, it's a secondary consideration." He picked up a pad and a pen from beside the telephone and began writing. "Ruskin rides a bicycle?" he asked without looking up.

"Not to say *rides*."

"He has no car?"

."His parents probably have one, but I've never seen him use it."

"Webber?"

"No car."

"What transport does he use?"

"His legs." He looked up. "I'm not being funny. He runs. Jogs. As far as I know, that's how he gets around."

"Grafman?"

"One car. Rented. The one that caused all the trouble."

"The man with laryngitis?"

"Persky. I assume no car, otherwise Grafman wouldn't have had to call a taxi the day Thea went missing."

"The botanical girl uses a bicycle?"

"Sarah. Yes. Exclusively, from what I've seen."

"And the man from the marina?"

"He might have a car. I've only seen him in Thea's. I mean Grafman's."

He nodded, and stared at what he'd written. He was rolling along now. Twenty mph, but it *was*, after all, uphill.

I said, "You left one out. And for all I know, he travels by helicopter."

"Who does?"

"The random psychopath." I didn't believe in him, but I had to put him to rest.

"There was no random psychopath. The girl wasn't molested. She wasn't bludgeoned, strangled, knifed, or shot. Granted, I find it difficult to keep abreast of the latest tools in the homicidal arsenal, but by and large the unpremeditated act of a random killer leaves a mark." He took my map of the island from the coffee table to the dining table. "This death was planned. A vital part of that plan was to take the girl to a secluded area of the Refuge when she was already dying, and leave her there, where she wouldn't be seen—and possibly saved—before whatever was killing her did its work. About as premeditated an act as possible." He unfolded the map. "And the girl was a visitor to the island. Over a week or two, unless she was spying for the KGB, she couldn't have made too many vindictive enemies among the locals. Two is about the limit." He spread out the map on the dining table. "In addition to those two, there are four nonresidents whose lives she was currently affecting. For a simple girl from the Midwest, I'd say that generating strong feelings of one kind or another—in six different people at the same time—is as much as you can expect. That gives us six possibilities." He stood over the map, leaning on the palms of his hands.

"Six or eight or a thousand, if it was premeditated, the killer had to have a *motive*. So *why* is the Gasparilla business a secondary consideration?"

He pointed to a spot on the map. "That's the Refuge?" I nodded. "Show me the location of the restaurant where you last saw that group together." I pointed. "And the hotel where you delivered the girl's car keys." I pointed again. He drew a triangle with his finger. "Miles apart. And only one known car and two bicycles among the six of them. With the most compelling motive in the world, in order to hide a body in the Refuge, you first have to *get* there."

CHAPTER TWELVE

THE MORNING WAS STILL FRESH WHEN I LEFT THE APART-
ment. Hot in the sun but cool and fragrant in the shade. In my
shoulder bag was a list of questions to be answered, written in
Greenfield's fine inscrutable hand, legible to two or three people in the world, of which fortunately, I was one. Greenfield
himself I had left sitting on the balcony with paper and
ballpoint, thinking.

Beginning at the top of the list, I went along the landing and
tapped at Ruskin's door. When it was opened, it was Webber
who stood there. We stared at each other for a moment, both of
us taken aback. Webber was barefoot and holding a glass of
iced tea. After the initial jolt of surprise he avoided my eyes.

"Sherm went down to the office for a minute," he said.

"Oh, I murmured, and stepped into the apartment. "I was
just wondering if he'd heard anything more—" I looked
around. The furnishings had come intact from Great Neck or
Teaneck or some suburban Neck: French provincial, with lots
of hard little throw pillows on the sofa, stereo built into a bookcase, forty or fifty framed photographs standing about, mostly
of the same three children at successive stages of growth, one

of a younger Sherman, a wedding picture in which he looked defiant in the company of a forthright, clever-looking woman. "—anything more," I concluded, "about what killed Thea."

Webber had plunked himself down on the sofa, very much at home in a truculent sort of way, still not looking at me, studying his iced tea with remarkable interest. "We haven't heard anything. I spoke to Grafman this morning, but he didn't mention it. In fact, all he said was there was no reason for him to go on picking up the tab for two extra rooms. Sherm is letting me stay here."

"I see."

"Alvin's staying at Grafman's."

"Oh yes?"

"Luckily, because he's sick as a dog."

"Which dog?"

He looked at me *then*, all right, but quickly returned to his iced tea.

"I'm sorry, that simile always bothers me. What's wrong with—um—Alvin? His laryngitis develop into something?"

He shrugged. "Says he has a violent headache and a sore throat."

"He's had a bad time here."

"Who hasn't."

"How is Mr. Grafman taking it?"

"Grafman." He swished the tea in his glass. "Who knows how Grafman feels about anything. He's a pragmatist, I guess. Anyway, he's getting rid of reporters and trying to track down her family. Someplace in North Dakota or somewhere."

Minnesota, Gary. You're too self-absorbed, you don't listen.

"I thought I saw them jogging on the beach. Alvin and Mr. Grafman."

"Grafman *jogging*?" He looked up, astonished, then shook his head and looked away. "It wasn't Grafman."

"Why not? He seems to be in good shape."

"He's got a paunch. Besides, he only exercises when he can win something. Tennis. He likes competitive sports. He couldn't run a quarter of a mile. Maybe Alvin could, but he's sick. Even a good runner wouldn't run when he's sick."

"How many miles do *you* do?"

"At home I do between twelve and fifteen. Here, not much. I haven't had time."

"This—tragedy—has been a double blow for you." His eyes flicked up, then immediately back to the tea. "I mean your work. It seems callous to think about Thea in those terms, but you'd be superhuman if you didn't." No response. "Does this mean the end of your project?"

"Maybe. Not necessarily. Like they say in baseball, it's not over till it's over."

"That's hopeful, then." I moved to the door and it occurred to me it might just be possible to do the investigation a service by lifting Greenfield's spirits an inch or so from the bowels of the earth. "We appreciate the music." I gestured to the stereo from which Kreisler's "Liebeslied" was currently dripping. "We have a guest from New York who can barely survive without it, and unfortunately my mother's stereo is in for repairs. I don't suppose—you don't know if—um—Sherman—by any chance—has some Mahler?"

"Mahler. No. I doubt it. Probably not."

I nodded and opened the door. "Well, let me know if you hear anything more."

"Sure. If we do." He watched his tea swirling.

I wondered, as I went down the stairs to where the car was parked, if not being able to look at the person with whom you are conversing is characteristic of your relatively modest murderer.

Down Periwinkle. Up the San–Cap road.

I turned into the Conservation Center and parked near the nursery. This would be my first encounter with Sarah McChesney since the discovery of the body. I found myself both alert and apprehensive: would she make a parade of fraudulent horror, or an equally suspicious display of indifference? If she pretended shock at the news, that would be worst of all. She might not own a television set, and she might not have seen a local paper, but word of mouth in this community must be supersonic. Oh Sarah, damn you, this trotting around is all your fault.

I left the car and walked down the path between the hundreds of small potted plants, taking time to stop and read the tags: wild olives, Peperomia, obtusifolia, as though, like any tourist, I'd come to visit the nursery. In the distance, busy at a potting table, I saw the nursery manager, the amiable woman to whom I'd spoken the other day. No sign of Sarah. But squarely ahead of me stood a large, rust-colored shed, and when I looked in, there she was, toward the back, hair in her eyes, slightly frayed jeans, a navy T-shirt on which a drop of bleach had apparently fallen, leaving a white medal permanently pinned over one breast.

She was hunched over a row of numbered feeding bins in which tiny animals were scurrying—mice or gerbils—her long, stained fingers tending, with infinite care, to the drip bottles that supplied them with water. The place was clean, tidy, organized—rakes, hoes and saws hanging neatly from hooks in the wall, ladders, sawhorses, wooden crates and smoothly cut planks stacked in one corner, shelves on which containers of Ortho spray, Malathion and plant nutrients were lined up along- side a row of emptied Planters Peanuts cans now used to store hammers, pliers, screwdrivers and nails. She looked up.

"Hi," she said, with no smile. "Hi," and wiped her hands down the sides of her jeans, looking over my shoulder.

"I was going to take the guided tour"—I gestured toward the trails beyond the Center building—"but I decided to start here. This is interesting. Looks like a research center."

"Research, plant propagation, educational facility. Indige- nous plants only. Native plants. That's the whole point. We try to educate people to landscape with native plants." She rattled it off, her voice pitched high, like a guide's. "Because this is a subtropical climate, you see, and when people bring in exotic plants, tropical plants, for color you know, splashy plants, it just throws off the eco system.Every landscape can be a small self-sustaining eco system if it's planted correctly." She marched out of the shed, along a series of screened divisions lined with tables covered with potted seedlings, adjusting the misters, lecturing, as though we'd never met before. "So that's what we do, we gather information on their growth habits, the native plants, and we have plant digs, we go to undisturbed places, wild places, and take cuttings, and collect seeds off trees and shrubs and get them to germinate, and try to educate the public to plant *communities* of plants, so they'll support each other, because *imported* plants don't do that, they need special attention, they need extra watering, they use up our resources, the native wild plants can survive without doing that. It's a philosophy, you see, the native-plant movement. You know she's dead?''

She stopped in her tracks and stared at me with huge gray eyes, no longer the guide but the quivering doe I remembered from our first meeting.

"Fat Cat. She's dead. I shouldn't call her that, now that she's . . . she died in the Refuge. She's dead." Her sharp-nosed little face seemed paler than usual and her eyes darted around as though death might be lurking in the immediate vicinity, waiting to pounce again. Or as though the law might be after her.

"I heard about it," I said. "It was a shock. Tragic." I made a show of looking around at the seedlings. "It's odd what shock does to you. My first reaction was to wonder if you managed to get your pictures before it happened."

She looked at me blankly, as though I'd said something incomprehensible. Then, "Oh. I told you about that, didn't I?" She busied herself moving the plants around. "No. I never saw her. I didn't see her at all. She never showed up."

"Where?"

"Where—?"

"Where didn't she show up?"

"Oh. At the marina. I expected her to come to the marina. To pick up Leroy. But she didn't. I was going to follow them. They might not have gone to the property. They could have gone anywhere. Bowman's Beach. Or up Dinkin's Bayou to Wulfert. But she didn't show up. I waited at least an hour."

"I suppose you'd have seen if he took his own car and went to meet her."

"He couldn't. They suspended his license. He speeds a lot."

"How does he get to work? Does he run?"

"Not Leroy. He only moves on wheels. Not a bicycle, though. On no, that's not macho enough for him. It would destroy his image. I think he gets a ride with one of the other men at the marina."

"So he was there at the marina all the time you were there?"

"He was there, all right."

I nodded and looked away, at the seedlings. " Upset when she didn't show up?"

She had picked up a pot and was examining the underside of

the plant, frowning at it. "Well, I wouldn't ask him, would I? I was keeping out of sight."

I meant you, Sarah. Were you upset? Or weren't you there? "Why do you suppose she didn't come?"

She shrugged impatiently, as though the vagaries of human relationships were supremely unimportant. Her nervous eyes raked the horizon. "They don't know what she died of, you know. I had that from a reliable source. They can't tell what it was. They might never find out. A person is alive and suddenly they're not, and that's all there is to it. Gone. Like those fish on the beach. Except they *know* what killed the fish. But the fish are just as dead, whether they know or not." Suddenly she shook hair out of her eyes, started back to the shed, and in a voice that had just a shade of calculation to it, she said, "He wanted to take her out on a boat. Leroy. I heard them the other day on the beach at the property. He wanted to run a boat over to The Gulls and pick her up. She said if he did that she'd pretend she didn't know him, and she wouldn't see him again. I didn't think, at the time, that she meant it, but maybe that's what happened." She snorted. "That would be a slap in the face for the Great Lover!"

Sarah stopped at the entrance to the shed, a clear indication I wasn't to follow. Then, with a look of surprise and relief, as though she'd solved a knotty problem, she reached out one long, thin arm and touched my elbow with her grubby fingers. "She was an import. An exotic plant. She didn't fit into the eco system." She nodded to herself and disappeared into the shed.

I went back to the car wishing she hadn't come up with that metaphor and wondering if everything she'd told me was fabrication—going to the marina to wait for Thea, Leroy wanting to take a boat to The Gulls, all of it. Guileless she wasn't. On the other hand, she'd seemed genuinely upset, as though she'd gone after a stray animal with a stick to chase it away from the sea oats, only to find it had run into the Gulf and drowned.

But why had she answered the wrong question?

I took a deep breath, unfolded my map to find the location of the marina, and swore out loud. Sanibel Marina, Blind Pass Marina, Tarpon Bay, South Seas . . . it would take days to check them all. Why hadn't it occurred to me there'd be more than one? I could hardly go back to the shed with some devious device for finding out which one I wanted. Take a random shot?

Geography decided me. Tarpon Bay was the closest. I left the Conservation Center, made a right turn and subsequently a left, and eventually found myself at the water's edge, surrounded by a small army of pelicans.

They waddled up and down the boardwalk that led to the pier, big bodies on absurdly short legs, beaks like huge gardening shears seen sideways, both silly and menacing. A few visitors stood nearby, grinning at them foolishly and taking snapshots. Beyond them two skiffs tied to the pier were moving in a gentle swell of bay water, and a sunbrowned boy with straw-colored hair was hosing down a gleaming cruiser. That was as good a place to begin as any, but between the sand where I stood and the boats bobbing in the bay were the pelicans. They looked hungry. I'd heard they ate twenty percent of their body weight in food every day. Could one get from here to there without being mistaken for a fish?

A couple emerged from a shed in which, according to the signs, one could either rent a canoe or buy pelican food. The woman held a brown paper bag, and the pelicans, as one, turned and advanced on her. While she nervously dispensed the pelican food she'd bought, I slipped past and approached the cruiser.

"Excuse me—" The boy looked up, narrowing his eyes against the sun. "You work here?" He nodded. "Do you know if anyone happened to find an ivory bracelet on one of the boats earlier this week? I believe I lost it around here somewhere. A carved ivory bracelet."

He shook his head. "You better ask in there"—he indicated the building that housed a fish market.

I ignored this. "It was Tuesday afternoon. I was watching one of the men who work here—um—he was cleaning up one of the boats. Dark-haired man, about thirty?"

"I don't know, ma'am, you—"

I described Leroy. More or less.

"Sounds like it could be Leroy, but—"

Right the first time. "Is he here now?"

"I haven't seen him. He could be out with a party."

Please let him be out. "Well—if he's the one—do you know if he was here Tuesday afternoon?"

He shook his head again. Sheepish smile. "You better ask inside."

I thanked him, made my way circumspectly past the pelicans and into the store, and found myself in the midst of stacks and racks of sailing gear and sportswear. Crepe-soled deck shoes, sweat shirts, canvas hats, heavy-weather slickers. The fish market, I gathered, was on the other side of the building.

Behind a counter a man in checked shirt, with a rugged, furrowed face, made change for a customer. He had the look of someone who knew his way around the premises, someone who'd been there for years, seen them come and go. I repeated my story about the bracelet.

"Tuesday." He uttered something between a snort and a laugh. "There's been a couple of hundred people through here since Tuesday—"

"I only missed it this morning, and I remembered the last time I'd worn it was the day I came here. I was out on the dock watching one of the men working on a boat. We've been thinking of chartering a—a party boat." A small orgy, actually. "I asked the man if I could see the cabin and he let me on board for a few minutes, and I remember when I was on board noticing the catch of the bracelet was open. I thought I closed it but it could easily have falled off. On the boat. I—"

A woman holding a T-shirt stamped with the word *Sanibel* took precedence over my problem. and I waited while she paid for it and went off.

"I thought if the man who was working on the boat happens to be around, I could ask him. Someone out there suggested it might be a man called Leroy—"

"He wouldn't keep the bracelet." Shortly.

"I'm sure he wouldn't. I just—"

"He's one of our captains. He's new, but we don't hire the kind of people who—"

"No, of course not. I thought he might have put it aside, in a safe place, thinking I'd come back for it. Or until he had a chance to bring it in here. And then forgot about it. If he's around, I could—"

"Not here right now."

"But he *was* here on Tuesday? Because it *could* have been someone else. I only remember vaguely what he looked like. But it was definitely Tuesday afternoon, so whoever was here then—"

With the expression of one performing an act of futility, he reached under the counter, brought forth a loose-leaf notebook, fingered through the pages.

"Tuesday," I repeated helpfully, "between—let's see— sometime between two and three-thirty."

He ran the reverse tip of a ball-point down the page. "Tuesday morning he went out with a fishing party. Checked back in at one P.M."

"Then he *was* here."

The man shook his head. "He had the afternoon off. Nobody hangs around on their day off. Especially not Leroy."

"But—he must have stayed to clean up the boat—"

"That boat went out again at one-thirty. In fact"—he looked back at the page, and then at me, with dawning curiosity—"all of our boats happened to be out just then, except the ones in storage. And we had no order to clean up any of those." He watched my face closely, doubtless wondering if this was the notorious lost-bracelet racket and I was going to claim it was worth a fortune.

"I could be wrong about the time," I said, frowning. "I'll have to check with my husband." I turned away, and then back again. "In case we decide on that party boat do you have a list of your rates?" Avert suspicion whenever possible. He added some figures to a flyer printed with tide tables, handed it to me, and I went to the doorway.

A phalanx of pelicans barred the way, spreading aggressively across the exit. I stopped, trapped. Short of levitation I could see no way of getting past them. They stood there in closed ranks, pointing their huge bills at me as though the bills were spears. A cold-eyed gang, if ever I saw one. I might be there yet if a man carrying a brown paper bag hadn't appeared around the corner of the building. Any brown bag looked good to them; they went after him.

As I slunk out of the doorway an open fishing boat chugged in to the pier and a bronze god with dark hair shut off the motor, hopped out, tied it up and helped a middle-aged couple disembark amid a mass of fishing gear. Leroy.

The middle-aged man clambering out looked tired. His wife looked excited. She wore denim shorts and a lot of streaked hair that fell straight and simple at fifty dollars a cut, and when she used Leroy's outstretched hand to step onto the pier she fell quite deliberately against him, gluing her thin cotton-knit Saks shirt to his chest long enough to raise any eyebrow that might be passing. Leroy treated her to his white-toothed grin, set her straight and moved lithely down to the deck to retrieve a carry-all, brown arms gleaming, broad shoulders and narrow waist turning in one effortless move as he handed it up. No question he was wearing clothes, but I'd be at a loss to describe them—clothes disappeared on him, the body eclipsed mere fabric. The woman, reaching down for the bag, all but launched herself off the pier to fall upon him once more. Understandable. Even at fifty yards' distance the sheen of the perfect stallion was unmistakable and potent. Quite an asset for a boat-rental operation. No wonder they sprang to his defense.

When finally the woman joined her tired husband on the boardwalk, her face was sulky with reluctance. They came toward me, heading for the parking lot, and not far behind came Leroy. Strutting sexuality on the hoof. Before I had the presence of mind to turn away, our eyes met, and his reminded me of the pelicans': inward-focused and pitiless.

I wasted no more time getting to the car and away from the marina before he could hear the bracelet story. Gloomily I turned left on the San–Cap road. The fact that Leroy had been gone from the marina on Tuesday afternoon was not an unmixed blessing. Put him squarely on the list, maybe, but gave me a choice as to which lie Sarah had told. Had she covered for Leroy? (And if so, why?) Or had she never been at the marina at all?

I turned in at the bicycle-rental office on Periwinkle that was all but hidden in the sea of wheels and orange flags that surrounded it. The young woman working there was, on the contrary, out in full view. What little skin was covered by the green tank top was adequately outlined beneath it. She was short as well as nubile, with a sweet round face and wire-framed eyeglasses. In the thin, slightly off-pitch voice of a precocious eight-year-old, she asked if she could help me.

"I have a rather strange problem." Assuming an embarrassed and conspiratorial air. "I met these three men on the beach, oh, about a week ago." Immediately she was interested. "They've been, well, *bothering* me. Or *one* of them has. Leaving notes under my door. You know. Suggestive." The big eyes behind the glasses were riveted on my face. "It's really beginning to upset me, and I think I should make a complaint to the police, but the trouble is I don't know which of the three is doing it, and I don't want to accuse an innocent person." She shook her head, vehemently agreeing. "All I know is that he rides a bicycle. Once it was a moped. Each time he delivers a note, he knocks at the door and disappears, and when I look out all I can see is the back of this figure, riding away. In the dark. He always delivers the note at night. So I can't tell which of them it is. Now, they're all tourists, visitors, so the bike and the moped must be rented. I have their names, so—if I could find out which one of them did the renting—"

Was I ever young enough, I wondered, to swallow a story like that?

"That's crazy," she breathed, "but I've heard worse than that. There are all kinds of weirdos around."

"That's why I want to find out. If you could check for me—"

She pushed the glasses back on her nose. "I'll have to have your name and where you're staying." She was apologetic. "I can't give out information to just anybody."

I complied.

"And what's the date?"

"Which date?"

"The day he rented the bike. Or the moped."

"I suppose it could have been anytime in the last ten days or so."

"Ooooh." The little mouth turned down at the corners, offering condolences. "That's a problem. We've got *thousands* of waivers filed away. I couldn't go through *all* of them. If you could tell me what day to look through, see, they're filed by the day."

Oh lovely. And what if I picked the wrong day? "Try last Tuesday."

"Tuesday." She checked a calendar, drawing her tiny eyebrows together, the tip of her tongue peeking from the corner of her mouth. Wrote the date on a slip of paper. "And the names?"

I added *Grafman, Webber, Persky* to the slip of paper. and she took it with her to the file cabinets. After much peering and mumbling and running the tip of her tongue back and forth over her upper lip, she returned, shaking her curls sadly.

"Nope," she said, "sorry. You want to try another date?"

I sighed. "I wouldn't know where to begin."

"I wish I could help you but, see, that's the system. Somebody comes in, wants a bike for an hour or maybe the whole day—or a moped—we copy their driver's license on the copier and they sign the waiver and we file it away under the date, and that's all the record there is."

An hour or maybe the whole day. Something Ruskin had said came back to me. Maybe I'd come to the wrong place. "You don't rent anything for more than a day at a time?"

"Oh sure. But if they want it longer than that, anything overnight, say, or three days, or a week, then we keep a double check, we record it in the— Oh! The black *book*!" She might have been granted a revelation as to life's most puzzling question.

"Would it be a lot of work to check that, starting ten days ago?"

"Nothing *to* it!" She looked around. "Black book, black book. I'm just helping out today, see, this isn't my regular job." She found a black clipboard folder, counted back ten days on the calendar with a pudgy little finger, and began the painstaking search. After giving the tip of her tongue a lot of exercise, she closed the folder and looked up dolefully. "I'm really sorry. You could try next door."

I thanked her, palmed the slip of paper with the three names on it—no sense leaving that around—and another possibility occurred to me. "What happens if someone comes in for a rental and doesn't have a driver's license?"

"We take their name and home address and where they're staying on the island. People here are pretty honest. Especially when they know we can check by calling the place where they say they're staying.''

As I left, two refugees from John Cheever country came in, fit and blond and immaculate in tennis clothes, the kind who seem to have a built-in repellent to dirt or grime or grunginess of any kind. People like that, I thought, never have to carry an ID. They could rent a yacht for a month on the strength of their impeccable turnout.

Yet I heard her ask for a driver's license. What's the world coming to?

The other bicycle rental, a stone's throw away, was equally fruitless. There had been no rentals to anyone named Grafman or Webber or Persky.

As I pulled away from the field of pennant-decorated bikes, I wondered fleetingly if a painstaking search of several acres of Refuge would disclose a small orange flag that was supposedly knocked off by a vicious fence.

Time to report back to Mission Control.

CHAPTER THIRTEEN

IN THE ARCADE THAT SHADED THE FAÇADES OF THE PALM Ridge shops from the hot sun, Greenfield placed his container of lemonade by his side on the bench and, with no attempt to conceal his pessimism as to the outcome, bit into a chicken-filled croissant. Pastry flakes scattered far and wide. His glance at me conveyed that beside his own trials, those of the combined Christian martyrs were as naught.

"It's worth it," I assured him, "these croissants are world-famous." And for all I knew, they might be.

The *al fresco* lunch had been prompted by the appearance at our front door, shortly before my own return, of Mother's small friend with the thinning red hair, whose faded eyes, on being introduced to Greenfield, had lit up, apparently, with unmistakable avidity. "Such a *lovely* man," she had chirped to me, while my mother looked bored. (*She* knew better: provocative, maybe, lovely, no.) Greenfield had fled to the Sea Grape grounds, where he sat in the shade of a pepper tree, presumably thinking and getting hungry, until I arrived and conveyed him to the arcade. I had no time to waste on restaurants. Monday was not far off.

He listened while I reported my findings. Drank lemonade for a while. Looked as though he were trying dutifully to remember what it was he was supposed to do with the information. Finally put the container on the floor at his feet where a wasp immediately came to investigate it, and took a notebook from his pocket. He flipped the pages to one headed TUESDAY, and stared at it.

"It was close to two o'clock," he said, "when you saw that group in front of the restaurant."

"Quarter of two when I went into the restaurant. They were leaving then."

"And it was four-thirty when you got to Grafman's hotel with the car keys."

"Give or take a minute. I was worried about getting back to the Sea Grape, so I looked."

We've been all over this, Charlie. Let's get on with it.

He flipped to the next page, studied the six names written there, removed a pencil from its niche in the spine of the notebook and crossed off one of the names. I leaned over to see which one.

"*Grafman?* You're crossing off *Grafman?*"

"You tell me"—he brushed flaky crumbs from his lap—"how he got from the restaurant to the Refuge, and back to his hotel, allowing time to find the girl and decoy her out to that isolated spot, in two and a half hours, with no car, no bicycle or motor scooter, and, according to Webber, who knows about such things, not enough stamina to run a quarter of a mile."

"We haven't exhausted all the possibilities."

"For instance?"

"A taxi."

"You go on record that Grafman is mentally impaired?"

Oh. Well, on second thought. *Driver, take me to the Refuge and keep the motor running, I won't be long.* No, I suppose not. "He could have rented another car."

"Then why didn't he have one at four-thirty, when you brought him the keys to the first one? And if he had, whose license did he use when he rented it? The idea of checking all rentals for that day wouldn't necessarily begin and end with us. And a man like Grafman is perfectly capable of anticipating police interest in the sudden acquisition of a second car."

"Then there must be another answer."

"Come up with it and I'll put him back on the list." His pencil went to the next name. "If Webber is a practiced runner he could certainly do ten miles or so in that time, with a half-hour to spare. When you saw him at four-thirty, did he look as though he'd been running?"

"He *always* looks as though he's been running. He *is* always running. He runs when he *sits*."

He moved on to the next name. I anticipated him.

"Persky," I said impatiently, "didn't look as though he'd been running, but he's one of those people who always look freshly laundered. I saw two of that breed at the bike rental. Anyway, Persky—"

"Had every reason to want the girl alive." The pencil moved. "Whereas your friend Ruskin"—he circled the name— "not only had a bicycle, but happened to be riding it in the vicinity of the Refuge at a very convenient time."

"Actually he was some distance from the Refuge when I saw him. Just up the road here, in fact. To be perfectly fair, he could have been coming from the Conservation Center."

Unless, of course, there's an orange flag somewhere in the Refuge.

He shot me a quizzical look. "You know there was a nineteenth-century writer called Ruskin. An art critic and social reformer. He went mad." He went back to his list.

"The botanist. McChesney," he said.

"Sarah." It took him a good few years to reach a first-name basis.

"McChesney," he repeated, "was also on a bicycle at the right time in roughly the right vicinity. What's more, she had no time limit unless she had to be back at work, and I gather that's flexible, and virtually next door to the Refuge. To top it off, she seems to have lied about something important." He circled the name.

I looked away and said nothing. What was this review all about anyway? Was it supposed to indicate his mind working? Coming to significant conclusions? Pitiful, if so.

"Finally," he said, "the man at the marina. Who, of course, had a very good way of getting to the Refuge."

"Leroy had a way?" More Greenfield flimflam. "*How*? He

had no license to operate a car or a moped, he can't ride a bicycle and he doesn't run. Admittedly, Sarah told me that, but I believe it because it fits the man. So what did he use, a balloon?''

"Maggie. This is an island.''

"What does that—'' It's astonishing how one overlooks the obvious. "My God,'' I said, "can you *do* that?'' I scrambled in my bag for the map, unfolded it. The island was bracketed on the beach side by the Gulf, on the Refuge side by Pine Island Sound, the body of water that separated it from the mainland. At the east end of the Refuge, Tarpon Bay flowed into the Sound. Greenfield drew a line from the Tarpon Bay Marina out to Pine Island Sound and from there into the lagoons that bordered the Refuge drive.

"A matter of minutes,'' he said, "in a motorboat.''

"I knew it!'' I looked up from the map, triumphant. "There you are! I knew there must be a way for Grafman to get there!''

Greenfield rubbed his nose thoughtfully. "I think I'm going to insist on meeting Grafman. From the prejudice he's inspired in you, he must walk around with a sheet over his head.''

"It's pure logic, that's all. First of all, he has a motive so ancient it's Biblical, and secondly, he came looking for me in the Refuge. Why did he do that? Why did he drag Webber over to Ruskin's to find me, and then come tearing out to the Refuge to track me down? Just to ask me if Thea had revealed her plans to me the day before? Come on, Charlie. He wanted to find out how much I knew. He was afraid Thea might have told me something: that he had threatened her or whatnot. He wanted to know if by some chance I'd *seen* him at the Refuge.''

"Why did he need Webber and Ruskin along for that?''

"I don't know. As witness to the fact that he was worried about Thea, that he was doing everything possible to find her. The hell he was. You should have seen him at the Indian mound. He all but bound me hand and foot to keep me from going out there.''

"From what you told me, the other two didn't think much of the idea either.''

I threw up a hand irritably. "Maybe they're all in it together. But Grafman got there by boat, that's how.''

"Make some attempt, Maggie, to bring your native intelligence to bear. If Grafman hired a boat, he'd still have to get to and from the marina, he'd have to be lucky enough to find a boat available exactly when he needed it, and he'd have to possess enough small-craft expertise to maneuver in strange waters."

"The marina also rents canoes. You don't need expertise for a canoe."

"This is a murder, not a Rudolf Friml operetta. Do you know how long it takes to paddle a canoe that distance? Not to mention that the trail he'd leave by renting *any* boat could only be more obvious if he marked it with reflectors. The one person who could use a boat without attracting undue attention is the man who works at the marina."

Leroy. I was silent for a while, thinking about Leroy. A cold, vain man. Physically strong. And a man who could easily be vindictive. Well, of course he was a possibility. If Sarah wasn't making up stories, and Thea really did let him know she could take him or leave him, the blow to his ego would have been shattering. He gets adulation from his female customers, he's probably been pursued and lusted after by half the local girls over the age of ten. He's a sexual sovereign. Then a real beauty comes along and dethrones him. "You're a pleasant pastime, Leroy, but don't push your luck." I could see the bad blood pounding in his arteries.

I brought my eyes back from the middle distance and saw that Greenfield was idly watching two men in the parking lot transferring fishing gear from the trunk of one car to the trunk of another. "So where does this get us, Charlie? What do we do next? It's Friday."

He put his notebook back in his pocket and stood up. "Why don't we go to that girl's place. McChesney." As though it seemed like a good way to pass the time.

From Grafman to Leroy to Sarah via everybody else. The man was taking potshots. Hoping to stumble onto something. Keeping me busy. Making it look good. I heaved a sigh and followed him to the car. "You mean the Conservation Center?"

"No, where she lives."

"She might not be there. I don't know how late she works."

"It's the place I want to see, not the girl."

The *place*! I got behind the wheel. "You don't mind if I ask why?"

"You told me," patiently, "that the girl who was killed knocked at your door at ten in the morning on Tuesday, looking for Ruskin, and at that point she was in good health. When you saw her again at two o'clock she looked 'a little queasy.' In the interim, according to the botan—McChesney—the group was having a picnic."

"I've never known a picnic where someone didn't come away queasy."

"There is, however, room for several Roman legions to march through, between *queasy* and *dead.*"

And what was he going to find on the beach next to Sarah's? Sand and water. "The picnic was four days ago. The police will have carted away the rubbish by now, if the group didn't."

"The police may not have been told about the picnic. It was illegal use of the property. A list of what the victim had to eat needn't be accompanied by the truth as to where she ate it. They ate by the side of a road somewhere. Garbage disposed of in some anonymous bin."

I stared across the street at police headquarters, quiet and trim on the outside. Was the inside a ferment of purposeful activity? Had they found anything? Did they have a clue? Or were they floundering like Greenfield, striking out in any direction that came to mind?

We drove.

"I suppose," I said, "there's no question she was poisoned."

"Unless you consider laser beams from a spaceship a serious possibility, I'd say the alternatives have been ruled out."

We passed the entrance to Bowman's Beach. We passed the Wulfert road.

I was going to follow them. They might have gone to Bowman's Beach or Wulfert. Sarah, in that shed, with all those containers of plant spray and Malathion and who knows what else. Weed killer. She wouldn't have to go far for poison.

"What about drugs?" I suggested hopefully. "This is Southern Florida, drug dealers outnumber the oranges. Thea wouldn't have taken anything voluntarily, but suppose someone slipped a fistful of something into her coffee? Or had a hypodermic handy and managed to—"

"Which of them would you say had access to controlled substances? Does anyone in that crowd seem likely to be an addict or a pusher? Not from what you told me.''

"Leroy could be a pusher. Easily. And he runs a boat.''

"Even if he handled the entire Afghanistan crop, I doubt there's a drug dose potent enough to kill, that would allow someone to function reasonably, including driving a car, for the hours that elapsed until she got to the Refuge.''

"What if he drugged her at the Gasparilla trail?''

He gave me a sidelong glance. No, of course not. She was glassy-eyed long before that. And I'd thought it was the heat. I shook my head, forbidding myself the ''if only's.''

We crossed Blind Pass and followed the Captiva road through the profusion of trees and bushes until we came to the gumbo-limbo. "This will be bumpy,'' I warned, but having survived the lurchings of a plane, Greenfield scarcely noticed the jouncing we took down the rutted track to Sarah's house.

There was no bicycle leaning against the side of the house. I called out, tooted the horn; no one came.

Greenfield got out of the car. "Which way to the beach?''

I balked at the thought of cutting across Sarah's garden, but the path through the ''property'' on the other side was intimidating. Evidently Grafman and company had found a way through to the beach, but playing trial and error in that mass of thicket and thorn was not an inviting prospect. I led the way to the back of Sarah's house.

Greenfield looked around with surprising interest at the nicker bean and wax myrtle and tamarind as we crossed the garden to the opening between the coco plum bushes. I was glad he was enjoying himself, wouldn't want the trip to be a *total* waste of time.

"Those are sea oats,'' I announced, pointing as I strode down the planks. "Don't touch. So. Here's the beach. The Grafman group would have been to the left.'' We walked over to where the adjoining property tumbled down to the sand in a wild jumble of bushes.

Between the bushes and the Gulf a detritus of charred branches and the ashes of a charcoal fire made a sooty splotch on the white sand. Greenfield walked around it slowly, examining it. There was nothing else to look at, except a few rotting fish at the tidemark.

I looked at the dead fish. Poison. Good God. Why hadn't I thought of it? So simple. So available. No hypodermic necessary. I looked over at Greenfield, mooning at the dead embers. So that's why he'd come here; to look for evidence of a fish fry.

"It never occurred to me," I admitted. "There it was, in plain view all over the island and I never made the connection."

"What are you talking about?"

"Red tide. A foolproof weapon. Just slip one of the dead ones into the pan and serve it to her—"

"Maggie. The reaction to red tide is immediate. The person has difficulty breathing, the lips and throat go numb, he or she has to be rushed to the hospital—"

"How do you know that!"

"Read your local paper." He picked up a charred branch from the ashes and examined it.

So he *had* no plan in coming here, after all. Just going through the motions. I sulked along the beach, looking at the shells. Good shelling beach. Lots of conches. I picked up a conch, gingerly. Another weapon. Who needed guns or knives? The island was liberally stocked with natural means for doing away with people.

Greenfield was walking around, looking down at the sand, kicking it, ignoring the shells, naturally, because he hadn't really come here to look for anything.

"Charlie." I held up the shell. "How fast is the reaction if you're bitten by a live creature from one of these?"

He looked up, returned to his sand scrutiny. "I don't know," he confessed. "But even if the murderer was expert enough to recognize a striatus shell, or a textile or a geographus, he hardly had time to go to the Pacific to pick one up. These aren't the deadly ones."

I dropped the shell. When did he manage to *read* so much! I turned and strolled back in the direction of Sarah's beach.

And Sarah erupted onto the sand.

At sight of Greenfield she froze. Eyes wide, nose quivering. Oh dear.

"Sarah!" I hoped my smile would pass for genuine. "Ah— I've been showing my friend around Captiva. Mr. Greenfield is . . . a friend of mine from New York. Um—an avid gardener. I told him about your garden and—ah—about the philosophy of landscaping with native plants. He was so . . . curious to see what you'd done here, I thought we'd take a chance that you'd be home and—''

"I don't like invasions," she said, "I don't like people tramping around. That's why we never had the road fixed. To discourage people from wandering in. You see what happens when people have access—!'' A furious gesture at the ashes on the "property" beach. "Coney Island. I can't have that. This is sanctuary.''

"My fault. I apologize,'' Greenfield said smoothly and looked at the ashes. "What were they doing, toasting marshmallows?''

"Frankfurters!'' she said, as though that compounded the crime. "Rolls! Mustard! Soda bottles!''

Greenfield shook his head sympathetically. "You have to bear in mind," he counseled, "that it's been an inequitable fight against the barbarians since the first tribesman despoiled the first oasis, and yet the trees are still here.''

What was that again about physicians and healing?

"I was hoping,'' he went on, overdoing it, "that Maggie could tell me something about the trees and plants you have here, but her memory is unreliable.''

Sarah's big gray eyes assessed him and relaxed, fractionally. Before long she was giving him the tour: inkberry, joewood, the lot, while Greenfield, nodding sagaciously, took notes as though acid soil and scales and double compound leaves were paramount interests in his life. When she offered us her gumbo-limbo tea, Greenfield the Fearless accepted. Why not? He was on holiday, after all.

Fingernails digging into my palms, I followed them into Sarah's house. The interior décor was not unexpected: spare and utilitarian except for a few framed pen-and-ink drawings on the walls, delicate sketches of trees and animals, and a few bunches of dried wildflowers in a variety of containers from expensive cranberry glass to plain jam jar. Scrubbed pine tables, large and small; flat, sailcloth-covered cushions on a plywood base for seating; linoleum in the kitchen and a far-from-new-stove.

The tea, though resinous, was not too bad taken in small sips, but watching her pouring it I found myself trying not to wonder if she brewed other concoctions there as well.

Greenfield, sitting on what looked like a hand-hewn chair at the kitchen table, had somehow taken on the rustic-cabin aura of the solitary outdoor man. A retired forest ranger, perhaps, man with an ax over his shoulder, walking the Trail of the Lonesome Pine. If I'd thought for a minute he had a plan, I'd have said he was working at disarming her. And succeeding.

"You stay here alone?" he asked.

"Some of the time." She put the teapot on a trivet. "My father can't stay when there's a red tide, he suffers from it. They're home in Massachusetts. My sister won't come here anymore since her little boy swallowed some rosary peas. They grow on vines, you know, in pea pods, and when the pods burst, there are these bright red seeds. She gave him pods to play with." She shuddered. "Luckily he swallowed a seed whole and didn't chew it. That's what comes of having no respect for nature. Nature is magnificent, not benevolent. There are—" She stopped, suddenly, tossed hair out of her eyes. "Anyway, my sister doesn't really like the island. She gets bored. She likes *cities*." She said it as one would say, "She eats leather."

She chattered on, about railroad cars rolling across the country full of ethylene gas to ripen the green fruit they transported, about pollution, about local fears for the future of the island with the enormous influx of people since the advent of the causeway.

"The traffic!" she breathed. "The traffic on this island, compared to what it used to be! A day doesn't pass when some oldtimer doesn't say, 'Let's blow up the bridge.' They say it as a joke, but I don't know, maybe it's the only solution."

I sipped my tea resignedly, convinced we were never going to leave. But Greenfield eventually stood up, made thank-you noises, and Sarah followed us out the front door, where her bicycle was once again propped against the side of the house, and watched as we got into the car.

I began to back down the track.

Greenfield indicated the path through the property on the left. "Does that go down to the beach?"

"I suppose it must. The Grafman group could hardly have cut across Sarah's garden."

We reached the road. "Pull off the track and leave the car here."

I hit the brake and stared at him. A *plan,* finally? "What do you mean, 'leave the car'?"

"Maggie."

I parked under the gumbo-limbo. "What—?" He got out and started back up the track. I locked the car and followed. "*Where* are you going? Charlie. What are you going to do?"

He motioned me to be quiet and trudged ahead until we were within yards of the clearing. Taking cover from the dense foliage on Sarah's side of the track, he went on cautiously to the point where it began to thin out, then, through the gaps, he scanned the house and the yard in front of it, nodded at me and crossed the track to the dubious-looking path that disappeared into the uncleared land. I hurried after him, worrying. What if we got lost in there and wandered around for hours? What if Sarah went out on her bicycle and saw the car under the gumbo-limbo? What if we got poison ivy? And what the hell were we doing, anyway? I butted my way through a network of vines, twigs, leaves, thorns, shrinking into myself to minimize contact.

"Charlie!" I croaked, trying to whisper and shout simultaneously. "What—?"

"Look for a branch," he said.

Look for *a* branch? Could he possibly have lost his reason?

"On the ground, discarded, one that's been stripped, with a charred tip."

Oh my Lord. I looked. I stumbled. I fought my way past low-lying limbs and treacherous roots, and emerged, finally, on the beach, without having spotted *a* discarded, stripped, charred branch.

"See if you can find it," he said, indicating the shrubs and bushes bordering the sand, "somewhere along here."

This is not a plan, I thought, this is the first sign that genius has crossed the threshold into madness. However, there are times when it's wiser to save your breath and humor such a person: occasionally what looks like madness turns out to be penicillin or the source of the Nile. I began peering into, under, and around the bushes, wondering if, in fact, anyone ever *had* found a needle in a haystack. Greenfield, beginning at the opposite end of the designated beachfront, proceeded to break off branches from whatever was growing there. I chose not to wonder about that. I cast frequent nervous glances toward Sarah's portion of beach, but she didn't appear.

When I'd covered half my assigned area, I straightened momentarily in deference to my back muscles, and saw Greenfield tug something out of the sand. I went over to him. In one hand he was holding a bouquet of leafy branches, in the other a single stripped branch with a charred top.

"It was thrown toward the bushes," he said, "but it fell short and landed in the sand. Dug itself in, like a penknife into wood."

"Good," I said, "let's go."

But he continued breaking off the odd branch from the bushes at my end until he ran out of jungle.

"Cuttings?" I asked, in dulcet tones, "for your garden?"

He started back through the wooded property, along the miserable path. "If nature, as your friend remarked, is not benevolent," he said, "then it bears investigation."

So that was the plan. Investigate the flora, they could be killers. Perhaps we could open a lab and analyze every specimen on this property *and* Sarah's. Rosary peas were probably the least of it. God knows what the wax myrtle would do to you, or the bay cedar, or the wild lime. And why stop with *this* territory? There was a whole island rampant with vegetation that we could investigate. We could be at it for years. Branches, for heaven's sake. When in doubt, look for branches.

We wrestled our way back to the track, made it from there to the car without incident, and he deposited his branches on the floor in the back.

Surveying the array of scratches on my bare arms as we rolled toward Blind Pass, I said, "I hope that discarded, stripped, charred branch turns out to be worth it, Charlie. I wouldn't want to pry by asking why it should."

"It's suggestive," he said calmly, "when the ashes of a picnic fire at which four people have been roasting frankfurters, contains only three charred branches." He took his notebook from his pocket and studied the scribbles he'd made in Sarah's garden. "It's even more suggestive when the missing branch proves to be the only one with not one but *three* notches cut into the business end."

CHAPTER FOURTEEN

"**S**TOP AT THE CONSERVATION CENTER."

I nodded. I'd decided to stop gnashing my teeth over Greenfield's haphazard methodology. If my pessimism proved justified, I'd have lost nothing, not even time, because I'd never known him to be dissuaded, even from a charade. If unjustified, I'd have saved the time it took for me to question, and Greenfield to be evasive. So I nodded, drove, stopped at the Conservation Center.

"There was an article in the local paper by a naturalist who seems to be an expert in these matters." He climbed out. "This should save you having to track him down."

I nodded.

"When you become speechless, I have to assume you're on the verge of collapse. You'd better wait here."

I nodded. He went off up the ramp.

The sense of moderate grunginess I'd had a few hours earlier had ripened, what with tramping around hot beach and through prickly woods, into a depressing feeling that my skin had been painted, head to toe, in something viscous. I vowed that when we got back to the Sea Grape, neither fire nor flood nor police with sirens wailing to nab me for further questioning would keep me from the pool.

Greenfield returned for his branches, disappeared once more up the ramp, and finally came back, empty-handed, and got into the passenger seat.

"The man's expected," he said. "I left a note."

I nodded. *What man? What note? What for? Never mind.*

In twenty minutes I was at the pool. Greenfield had, of course, neglected to bring swimming attire, given the mood of devout masochism in which he'd arrived, but when I'd cased the pool from the apartment window and pointed out that I would be having company from the next-door apartment, he'd decided to join me as a spectator.

Webber was climbing out of the pool when we arrived, and Ruskin's whale-like lashings were bringing him massively to the end of his stint. He lumbered out of the pool after Webber and they both registered our presence. Ruskin approached first, rubbing himself with a towel. I performed introductions.

"I understand you're a Mahler fan," Ruskin twanged.

"No," Greenfield replied dryly, "Yankee."

Ruskin's eyebrows climbed his forehead.

"Mahler has devotees," Greenfield added, "or detractors. Not fans."

"You never heard of the Mahler Fan Club of the Musicians' Union? Mahler's very big with musicians. One performance of his eighth symphony and the entire national membership is employed. They're all devoted fans. So is the International Association of Vocal Artists."

"And Alvin," Webber put in.

"Alvin," Ruskin said acidly, "Alvin is a money fan. A power fan."

"Alvin's great-grandfather," Webber retorted, "was with the Philharmonic when Mahler was over here conducting! Alvin wrote his college thesis on Mahler!"

"He's a Mah-ler schol-ar," Ruskin drawled. "I wish I had a dollar/For every moan and holler/From a Mahler/Scholar."

Webber turned his back on Ruskin and asked Greenfield, "Are you a musician?"

"I'm a newspaperman."

Ruskin leaned forward. "Webber here is a composer. He's just completed a magnificent score for a moribund musical."

"Why moribund?" Greenfield asked.

I slipped into the pool and swam, energetically, fighting off the demons. Exercising them out of my system. Exorcising them. Banishing speculation as to why Greenfield was engaging in showbiz chitchat. The water was crisp, the pull of it against my arms was a tonic, my legs flipped tirelessly, churning the water behind me. I could have gone on kicking and cleaving the water for hours.

But I climbed out, eventually, and found the three of them still talking, Ruskin slumped in an adjoining deck chair, Webber sitting on the leg rest facing Greenfield.

"Fate seems to have gone to great lengths," Greenfield was saying to Ruskin, "to solve your problem."

"I had no problem," Ruskin said. "I was out of it. I put it to Grafman that if he was going to build the show around Thea—nice girl, by the way, I mean that, I liked her, but she would have sunk us—if he was adamant about that, then I was out. He could have my script—what the hell, it was written, what was I going to do with it, wallpaper the den? Besides, Webber here"—he patted Webber on the back with more than a suggestion of irony—"Webber here had a big stake in Grafman, Grafman being the first producer in twenty auditions who came up with an offer. Webber is young, he'll learn, but I remember what it was like. At his age I seriously considered becoming an electrician just so I could put my name up on a marquee for five minutes. And of course we have an agreement. Right, Gary? We both signed a collaboration agreement before a word or a note was written, spelling out who gets what—money, billing, approvals, all that nice stuff. Subsequently, a Guild contract with Grafman, all percentages, obligations and perks laid out. Then Grafman made it an unwritten condition that Thea would play the female lead. Nobody had to draw any diagrams, the man was doing the show to keep this girl where he wanted her.

In writing we had cast approval, in real life it was take the girl or he'll cut his losses and we'll have no producer.''

Why was he telling Greenfield all this, I wondered, now that I had no water-cleaving to keep the demons at bay.

"Webber found it in his heart to accept the condition," Ruskin went on, "so fine. I wasn't going to spill blood in a lost cause, but if they wanted to give it a shot with Grafman's girl, and nobody else was waiting around waving option money at us, what could I lose? If God was in a whimsical mood, granted them a miracle and it worked, I got my percentage. If not, at least I'd still be alive. Which would not have been the case, Greenfield, if I'd stuck to it through the rehearsals and revisions and mayhem and havoc that goes on even when things are *perfect*. Believe this if you never believe another thing: trying to make that nice girl into a fiery Spanish princess bitch—that would *have* to be a three-heart-attack show." He zipped up his terry jacket. "So I had no problem. *Webber* had the problem: Mr. Alvin Persky, the Mahler devotee, Grafman's tame writer from that place in Southern California. You know anything about the Los Angeles entertainment mill?"

"I know," Greenfield said mildly, "that it's the only American industry engaged in the perfectly legal dumping of hazardous waste."

Ruskin cackled. Webber rubbed his hair sulkily with his towel. "Alvin's no dope," he protested, "and besides that, he has a musical background. Maybe not *Broadway* musical, but it means he has an ear, and that's important."

"Ears are good," Ruskin admitted, "but talent would be better. Luck, of course, is the best. And Persky is very, very lucky. He had to be, to be offered a first-class production without having a single theater credit."

"I'm surprised," Greenfield murmured, "that an experienced producer would take him on."

"I suppose you could say"—Ruskin scratched his sunburn—"that Grafman believes in encouraging young writers. But you'd be a lot closer to the truth if you said he likes to get people for the smallest possible advance."

"And he hired Persky to do what? You said the script had been completed."

"The book of a musical," Ruskin informed him, "is completed about seven minutes before the curtain goes up on opening night. The night after that you start rewriting all over again."

"Changes," Webber elaborated. "During rehearsal, scenes get cut, other scenes get put in, dialogue gets changed around, the writer has to keep working on it. Sherm wasn't going to be around, so we needed another writer. I think Alvin would have worked out."

Greenfield actually continued to look interested. "Then how did he constitute a problem?"

Simultaneously, Webber said "Points" and Ruskin said "Greed."

I watched Greenfield ostentatiously waiting for elucidation. What was going on here? What did this have to do with branches, or Sarah, or Leroy?

"There's a standard contract," Ruskin said. "Two, two and two. Percentages. Of the gross. Two percent for music, two for lyrics, two for book. Gary did both music and lyrics, so he was going to get rich. I, for my year of blood, sweat and doctor bills, was entitled to two percent. However, when I became a lameduck writer—no power, no presence, no rewrite—I agreed to hand over three-quarters of one percent to my replacement. Not only adequate, but goddam generous. Mr. Persky declined. In the words of Oliver Twist. In fact, Mr. Persky's demands began at outrageous and escalated to insane. Grafman would get Persky's agent on the phone in L.A., but Persky couldn't talk to him, with the laryngitis, he'd just listen and shake his head, and the agent finally said give him what he wants. If Grafman didn't have a time problem he would have sent him back to looneyland."

"But Mr. Persky got what he wanted?"

"More than once. Each success spawned another condition. He ended up owning everything but the scenery."

Webber scowled. "Come on, Sherm, he got one and a half percent, part of it from me."

"And my name off the script. I call that a good haul."

"What's the difference, nobody had a chance to sign anything. You've got it all back now."

"I'm not the only one who's got something back, kid."

Webber gave him a quick look that could have been rebuke or impatience, or even warning. Then he turned to Greenfield. "So if that's all right with you, I'll try to set it up with Grafman for tonight."

Greenfield nodded. *Set it up? It? What?*

Ruskin's sunglasses were studying me. "You're turning blue," he said, "not your best color."

Greenfield, alerted to the possibility that my damp robe was not sufficient protection against the evening breeze, examined me for signs of imminent illness. "If you were cold, why didn't you go in?"

"I was mesmerized." I turned to go. "Especially by the last part."

Greenfield got to his feet. A parting word. We cut across the lawn.

"So you acquired two buddies," I said interrogatively.

"I acquired information." He looked puzzled. "Ruskin interests me. Any man who claims to have devoted a year of his life to a piece of work and then given up, without much of a struggle, the right to call it his, is either an exceptionally independent spirit, or a simple liar."

"Mm-hm." That wasn't the aspect of the conversation that interested me. "What about this date you seem to have. What did you arrange for Webber to set up with Grafman?"

"I'm going to listen to Webber's score for the musical."

"The *score*? He's going to play the score for *you*? Who does he think you are?"

"A potential backer."

A backer. "For how much? Twenty-five dollars?"

"They somehow received the impression that I have unlimited funds."

Somehow! I could well imagine the casual allusions to his connection with NBC news, which, with a discreet manipulation of dates and emphasis, could transform his early career as a network news writer into a current niche high in the pantheon of communications media, somewhere between the publisher of the *Washington Post* and the president of RCA.

Why?

"Well, it's not going to happen," I said. "Grafman isn't going to let them come in there and use the piano. A musical soirée at a time like this: Sit there and listen to the songs Thea was supposed to sing? He couldn't!"

"Oh, I doubt that Grafman is a mass of quivering sensitivity. And he has an investment to protect."

"Not even Grafman is that callous." My mind rejected the picture of Grafman sitting in the palm-decorated armchair listening matter-of-factly to the music he'd bought to use as a bribe, for a girl who was dead. (Even if she was dead by his own hand. Especially then.) He'd have to walk out at the first note. He could do that, possibly, a businessman's compromise: let them use the place and arrange not to be there. Persky could let them in . . . . I stopped at the foot of the stairway. "Persky's staying there!"

"So you told me."

"Isn't that going to be *awkward*?"

"Ruskin and Webber seem able to cope with it."

I searched Greenfield's face for a clue, found only the slightly stubbly look of a man who hasn't shaved for ten hours. I'd vowed not to ask questions, but there was nothing in the vow about provocative comments. "Two days to go," I said, "and you're going to spend a whole evening listening to Webber's music."

"Webber's music," he started up the stairs, "is as sacred to him as the scarab to the Egyptians. His score was being dismantled, song by song, to accommodate the shortcomings of the girl who died. There's always the possibility that *that* is why she died."

"Ah-ha!" The dawn came up like thunder on the landing outside my mother's door and with it my staunch resolution to keep my mouth shut evaporated like the morning mist. "Now I *see* why Leroy's motorboat made it necessary for me to lacerate my skin looking for a branch!"

Greenfield was not only not amused, he was tired. "Under certain conditions," he said with finality, "the shortest distance between two points is a line that meanders." *J'y suis, J'y reste*. He went into the apartment.

Mother was watching the six o'clock news. The local television channel had been broadcasting daily reports based on whatever they could scrounge from the police that was even remotely connected with the business of the body in the Refuge: a single sneaker had been found at the base of the observation tower (it proved to belong to a child of four); a visitor from Omaha announced that he'd seen "a suspicious character" loitering around the Gasparilla trail that day (and accurately described a Refuge worker of unimpeachable character who had actually been on a completely different trail); an elderly woman claimed to have heard screams (but this was five miles away at the beginning of the Drive and the place had been full of shrieking birds). Today, it seemed, there'd been a belated response to the initial request by the police for information from anyone driving through the Refuge at the time who had seen anything unusual or picked up anyone walking the route.

"Some family," my mother told us, "said they'd given a lift to a girl who'd developed a blister. It fit beautifully into the time frame, but it turned out to have happened the day before."

"There weren't many people around that afternoon," I pointed out. If there had been, I thought, if only there had been . . .

At a quarter past eight that evening I was driving to The Gulls, Greenfield beside me, Webber and Ruskin in the back. Webber had indeed set it up with Grafman. Greenfield's mythical unlimited funds had outweighed Grafman's need to keep up appearances. This alone, I thought, should change Greenfield's decision to cross Grafman off the list.

Webber spent the ride gabbing nervously about an item he'd read in the *Times* concerning a new musical currently in out-of-town tryouts that was evidently based on Dreiser's *An American Tragedy*.

"Next year," Ruskin quipped, "the source material will be Kafka. Whatever happened to girls with garters on swings?"

Both voices were a bit shrill, a third or so off-center, as though they were trying to make sociable conversation while sitting on a backseat covered with tacks. They were definitely uneasy. It could be stage fright. It could be a subliminal awareness that the play's the thing a guilty conscience should avoid like the plague.

That, I told myself, was what Greenfield had in mind. Because he had to have *something* in mind.

Grafman opened the door to us. His manner was subdued, preoccupied, he had purple pouches under his eyes, deep lines bracketing his mouth. He sank into the palm-printed easy chair, exchanged opening remarks with Greenfield like someone too tired to bother parading his persona. If Greenfield had money, he wanted it, but not as much as he wanted the backing of a recording company or an oil consortium.

Webber, with a gesture of his head toward the back of the apartment, asked, "Is Alvin going to—?"

"He went to the movies," Grafman said.

"Oh, good. I mean, he must be feeling better." He sat down at the piano, spread out his music. Grafman took the phone off its rest. I waited for him to announce that he had an appointment elsewhere, but he simply sat there, waiting. A very thick hide, Grafman.

With Ruskin outlining the story as it developed between the musical numbers, Webber played the music and sang the lyrics, in a surprisingly true voice, with a great deal of unexpected charm and panache. It was a lively, melodious score, a little Bernstein here, a little Sondheim there, but a good deal of emerging Webber in between.

I watched them all closely for telltale signs: blanching, flushing, stammering, an uncontrollable licking of dry lips, but if guilt was revealing itself, it was either taking a subtler form than my eagle eye could detect or I needed to borrow a couple of eagles to supplement my limited vision. True, Webber was sweating prodigiously, but in Webber's case that, unfortunately, was merely normal. Ruskin alternately lounged on the sofa and loped around the room, his delivery of the narrative neither more nor less nasal than usual. Grafman sat through the performance as though he were conducting business in some foreign capital where he was at a disadvantage because of the language barrier: paranoia was predominant in his expression.

Even at the crucial moment, at the demise of the princess, there was no overt sign of undue stress. There's no business like Business.

After an hour or so, and a final dramatic solo, Gasparilla jumped into the Gulf of Mexico, the music crescendoed to a crashing dominant chord that never resolved to the tonic, and Webber swung away from the piano, palms out. "That's it."

Grafman replaced the telephone.

Greenfield made appropriate noises. There was a lot of talk about production plans. Webber volunteered that someone called Miguel Vanta had made a commitment to play Gasparilla. He said it as though he were throwing stardust in our eyes. The name was vaguely familiar to me; Greenfield probably associated it with a vineyard. Grafman mentioned a director he had lined up, and a set designer, "the only one who can handle a monster like this." But, he added, "who knows what their availabilities are, now that we have to postpone." And he looked away, at a hideous still life on the wall, of a cluster of shells that managed to look like maggots. "We have to recast the girl's part," he said tonelessly.

"So I understand," Greenfield murmured. "A tragic accident."

Grafman looked at Greenfield, then at me. Webber and Ruskin exchanged glances.

"Accident?" Grafman sneered. "Who knows? The goddam medical examiner doesn't even know what killed her. 'Death due to cause unknown.' What the hell does that mean? They can take pictures of an ant on Venus, but they can't figure out what killed somebody? 'Symptoms of gastroenteritis.' 'Nonspecific poison.' From what? She was with me all day. We ate the same food."

"The pathologist found nothing?"

"Ha! The pathology labs in this country! They've got evidence from nineteen sixty-*four* they still haven't touched.

Before a pathology lab gets around to running a test, the Palestinians will become *Quakers*!''

The tan of his face had become mottled. He pulled distractedly at his beard. Was he really in torment? could I possibly be wrong about him? I resisted the idea.

There was the sound of a key at the front door and Persky came into the room. Today, finally, he was wearing different slacks and a shirt I hadn't seen before. Ruskin gave him an evil grin. Webber went in search of a bathroom. The telephone rang and Grafman carried it out to the balcony. I wondered if decency would permit us to leave now that Greenfield had heard his score and learned whatever it was he'd come here to learn.

''How was the movie, Alvin?'' Ruskin asked. ''One of those digital-computer screenplays, isn't it? Machinery streaking across the screen, Superbeams chasing Ultraweapons, planets dissolving into subatomic particles, all that profoundly moving human drama?''

Persky smiled his small smile. ''Yes, it's an SFX film.''

''SFX?'' Greenfield looked as though he'd settled in for the night.

''Special effects,'' Persky explained in a hoarse voice. ''Very well done. Some spectacular mock-ups. These boys are really good. Of course they stole the main title business from *Superman*. You know: object shoots in from out-of-frame and resolves . . .''

''How is that done?'' Greenfield asked. Relaxed. A man with no pressing engagements.

Persky cleared his throat. ''You film with an open shutter on computer-assisted animation equipment, and when the object resolves, you combine it optically with SFX background footage . . .''

''Tell me about the movie,'' Ruskin urged. ''The story. Would you compare it to, say Balzac? Or is it closer to D.H. Lawrence?''

I thought it was a little tacky for Ruskin to keep battering away at Persky. Winners are supposed to jump over the net and shake hands, not throw the loser to the ground and pummel him.

"How was the acting?" Ruskin persisted. "Anything there for Olivier to worry about?"

Persky took a box of throat lozenges from his pocket and said quietly, "Magic isn't just for kids. It's an art form."

"Hell, yes," Ruskin said, "I love that stuff. But I miss the old days when it used to be the popcorn, not the main event. I guess when it comes to movies I'm just hung up on human beings. I grew up with them, you know. You get used to having them around."

Persky looked at him blankly.

"People, Alvin. You, me, Greenfield, the sexy lady over there. Flesh and blood, complexes and neuroses, triumphs and anxieties, love, hate. I like movies to be about people. Then you can throw in a little SFX for seasoning. Like the plague of locusts in *The Good Earth*."

Persky smiled. "Coffee grounds in a glass tank filled with water, shot with the camera upside down."

"Uh-huh. You remember the story? You remember the characters?"

"It was before my time."

Ruskin looked at him mournfully. "So were the coffee grounds."

Persky smiled innocently. "They certainly were. The technology's come a million miles since then. If those crews could see what we can do today! You ever see a computer constructing three-dimensional versions of an artist's sketch? Giving it shading, color, movement, any camera angle you want—" He coughed and popped a lozenge into his mouth.

"Charlie—" I said quietly, and looked pointedly at my watch.

He ignored it. "I understand," he said to Persky, "that in addition to your comprehensive knowledge of optical devices, you're an expert on Mahler."

Oh, Lord.

Persky turned to Greenfield politely, inquiringly. Then, modestly, he shrugged. "Not really."

"An enthusiast, then. You have a favorite among his works?"

Persky looked at the rug and thought about it. "It's hard to choose."

"The Twelfth Symphony, of course, is the masterpiece."

Greenfield, settling down for an amiable chat.

"Well—" Persky considered, "It's his more impressive piece of work."

"And the least impressive," Greenfield went on, "is the *Kindertotenlieder*. It's always a mistake to base your work on a subject alien to your own experience of life. A composer who's never had children, much less a child who died, should never have attempted to write those songs."

"We all make mistakes." Persky coughed again, persistently.

Grafman had come in from the balcony with the telephone and was conferring with Ruskin.

"Such a simple man, Mahler," Greenfield went on blithely, "placid, unadventurous. You'd never have guessed, from his personality, that he was capable of creating the kind of music he produced."

I stood up and moved pointedly toward the door, rattling my car keys. Persky kept nodding politely at Greenfield. Webber returned, gathered up his music and joined Grafman and Ruskin in a corner. It was another ten minutes before Webber and Ruskin said good-bye to Persky, who was evidently returning to California the following day. Webber looked confused, Ruskin jaunty. We piled into the Ford and headed for home.

"I need some milk," Ruskin said from the backseat. "Or tea, or Dr Pepper. Anything. No wonder Persky coughs, he probably hasn't been offered as much as a glass of water since he moved in there. Cheap, cheap, of all the producers in all the offices south of Fifty-seventh Street, we had to land the one with a time lock on his wallet."

Greenfield sat with his eyes half closed, watching the passing parade of dimly visible casuarinas, the warm breeze from the open windows ruffling his wispy hair. He said nothing until we were parting from the two of them on the landing, then he turned to Webber.

"You said Persky wrote a thesis on Mahler?" he asked.

"That's what Grafman told me."

"Grafman?"

"He got it from Alvin's agent. I suppose when the agent was trying to sell Grafman on hiring Alvin."

"You never discussed it with Persky himself?"

"We didn't talk much. He had laryngitis."

In the apartment, the lady of the house was sleeping peacefully while Romans in togas cavorted with goblets of wine on the television screen. I closed the bedroom door, returned to where Greenfield was standing at the glass doors looking out, poured two glasses of orange juice and said, "I don't know about you, but *I* didn't catch the conscience of any King."

He drank his juice, counted the stars, and replied, "That song the pirates sing, about Málaga, had four bars taken directly from Granados."

"Well, my God. There you are. It wasn't an evening wasted, after all. We may not have a bead on the killer, but we've certainly apprehended a thief."

He left the glass doors, subsided into the easy chair, rested his left ankle on his right knee. "I fail to see that it's a waste of time to learn as much as you can about your suspects. Persky alone would have been worth it."

"Persky! All I got from Persky was a headache. 'Animated computerized digitalized' whatever. You amaze me. Next thing you'll be spending all your time at a video arcade making green walnuts eat up blue walnuts."

"Maggie. I think it's time you did something about the gaps in your education."

"Gaps? Me? Not being informed about the latest technology is not a *gap*, it's a virtue!"

"How can you not know anything about the life of a man like Mahler?"

Oh. Mahler. "I know that Schubert and Schumann both had syphilis," I said defensively.

"Everybody had syphilis in those days."

"Liszt didn't. And I don't even like Liszt." Greenfield

closed his eyes, shutting me out. "All right," I said, "what about Mahler?"

"He never wrote a twelfth symphony: he didn't live long enough to complete number ten. He had two daughters and one of them died while she was still a child. And far from being placid, he is said to have been schizophrenic, sadistic, mercurial, charismatic, a man given to wild extremes of euphoria and gloom."

"Ah." I thought about that. "So Persky lied to his agent, about writing the thesis. He doesn't know beans about Mahler. He made it all up. Or his agent did."

"Whether it was Persky or the agent, it's a strange choice of lie. This was a Broadway producer he was trying to impress. He wasn't after a job as historian of the Vienna State Opera."

Who cares, I thought. What was the point of maundering on about Persky's peccadilloes, he'd wanted nothing but Thea alive and well so that he could start on the road to theatrical glory with this juicy plum of a job that had dropped into his lap. Greenfield was entertaining himself. This whole evening had been an exercise in musical one-upmanship. A self-indulgence. And tomorrow was Saturday.

I took an aspirin and went to bed.

CHAPTER FIFTEEN

THE NOISE WOKE ME: A NERVE-JARRING SOUND, AS though the Sea Grape were being attacked by a giant buzz saw. Blearily, I lurched to the window and looked out. A couple of maintenance men were busily hosing the walls of the next building with powerful jets of liquid from hoses attached to a portable and earsplitting machine.

"They're cleaning the buildings," my mother said resignedly, her eyes still shut.

"Good God. Why don't they just let it mellow with age?"

They'd chosen a perfect morning for it: humidity had crept bit by bit into the atmosphere during the night like the camel into the Arab's tent, finally taking over completely the space usually occupied by air. There was nothing to breathe but dampness. The bed sheets were damp, the breakfast toast was damp, the fluffy fresh towels from the Housekeeping dispensary became limp and soggy even as I carried them back to the apartment. Given those conditions, the additional water being supplied by the maintenance people seemed, to say the least, gratuitous.

Sealing the apartment with the air conditioning turned on and all the windows shut cut down somewhat on the noise and the perspiration, but only substituted claustrophobia. Greenfield did not like closed spaces. It was an act of bravery for him to enter an elevator. In a plane the lack of access to the open air only added cruel and unnecessary punishment to what was in any case a form of torture.

He prowled from the living room to his bedroom and back, made notes, looked at his watch, sighed often and deeply. Saturday morning, I thought, and where are we?

The fourth time he looked at his watch it told him, apparently, that the time was ripe, because he immediately went to the telephone, dialed a number and introduced himself to the party at the other end as Mr. Franklin. No need to look further than his middle name for the inspiration.

After a lengthy conversation he replaced the receiver. "The expert," he announced, "has examined the branches I left at the Conservation Center. All those with leaves on them are innocent. The stripped one with the three notches in it is oleander. In this context, deadly."

Deadly, I thought incredulously. Oleander. A lovely, decorative plant. Someone at the picnic had really given Thea an oleander branch. With three notches in it. Deadly, in this context. Three notches. To let the deadly sap escape? To identify it, make certain it went to the right person? And it did, and she skewered her frankfurter on it?

"Every part of that plant is potentially lethal," Greenfield added. "He advised me to get rid of the bush."

"What bush?"

"The one I mentioned in the note I left for the expert. The one growing near the house I recently acquired. From which someone had broken off that branch in preparation for a marshmallow roast. Fortunately I'm a cautious man and prevented its use until I could determine whether or not it was one of the toxic plants I'd heard about."

My mother, to whom this branch business was so much gibberish, gave me a guarded look.

"He had to invent some reason," I explained. "The man might have gone running to the police."

She looked, if possible, even more baffled.

Greenfield read from his notes. "*Symptoms include severe*

gastroenteritis, sweating, dilated pupils, dizziness, drowsiness, weakening heartbeat, possible coma, and a few other things. Compatible so far?''

"She was certainly sweating and dizzy, and I suppose her pupils were dilated. The police asked about drugs.''

He referred to the notes again. *"Symptoms begin several hours after ingestion.* That's what you noticed outside the restaurant.''

"She certainly wasn't her usual cheery self.''

"You said something about the ice cream.''

"It seemed to nauseate her. She complained they'd mixed pistachio in with the strawberry.''

"Xanthanopsia,'' he read from his notes.

My mother gave me another look.

"I never did get my degree in toxicology,'' I reminded him.

"The perception of objects as yellowish-green in color.'' He read on, *"Death usually occurs within a day,"* and dropped the notes on the coffee table. "Whoever arranged this has an unquestionable flair for painstaking planning. And a remarkable store of esoteric knowledge.'' He went to the bookshelves and scanned the volumes there.

"What—'' my mother began.

I forestalled her and said to Greenfield, carefully, "So. The deadly branch didn't come from any of those bushes at the beach. Someone brought it there.''

"Someone,'' he amended, "acquainted with its properties.''

Like, for instance, a botanist, I thought, feeling leaden. Obviously a botanist. Who else would have that "store of esoteric knowledge''?

Or would it be *common* knowledge to a native islander? Anyone living here long enough must of necessity learn the dos and don'ts.

Leroy.

"You realize,'' Greenfield said, leafing through one of the books, "this rules out the man from the marina. He'd hardly have been invited to that picnic.''

I clenched my teeth. There went Leroy, free to go on doubling the female pulse rate. While Sarah, by her own admission, had been on the beach. And could have wandered over, with that butter-wouldn't-melt smile of hers . . .

But she wasn't the only one there. Grafman, Webber . . .

"Ruskin and Grafman," I said, "were not on good terms. Ruskin wouldn't have been invited either."

"Unless the girl came to see him that morning to do just that. A peace offering." He closed the book and put it back. "There's no oleander in that plant book"—he frowned—"there are pictures of everything on earth that has a leaf and a flower, but no oleander. I'd like to be able to recognize it when I see it."

"Why?" my mother asked, finally getting a word in. "Are you planning a poisoning?"

Greenfield looked yearningly through the closed glass doors. "It had to be readily available to the person who brought it to the beach. There could be one, for example, in the grounds of The Gulls." I looked up: so he hadn't crossed off Grafman! "There could be one"—he gestured to the doors—"right out there."

"Ask Tom. The gardener. He's usually out there somewhere. He wears a blue cap."

Greenfield needed no urging.

I followed him. Up one path and down another, looking for Tom. As we neared the end of the grounds near the main entrance a clanging bell heralded the approach of the little red trolley, and it pulled up just ahead of us and waited while a panting woman with a straw shopping bag galumphed across the grass to board it.

Greenfield looked at the trolley and then at me. "Mass transport?"

I stared at the trolley. Bicycles I had investigated. Mopeds I had taken into account. Automobiles. I shook my head. "I forgot about it. I . . . absolutely . . . forgot about it. I don't know how it is we didn't pass one in the last few days, but we didn't and I forgot."

With admirable restraint he refrained from comment. His voice, however, at thirty-two degrees Fahrenheit, said it all. "Where does it go?"

"Back and forth." I gestured vaguely. The trolley bumped off down the street. "Probably going out to the lighthouse now."

"Does it have a schedule?"

"I suppose. Must have. I'll ask in the office." We turned back. "My God. Charlie. If it goes down Gulf Drive, and then up toward the Refuge, there's the answer. That's how Grafman got there!"

Impatient for the good news, I ran on ahead, found a stack of schedules in the office and brought one out to Greenfield.

There were two routes, one to the east end of the island, one to the west. On each route the trolley made over two dozen stops. On neither route did it go as far as the Refuge.

Greenfield folded the schedule, handed it back to me, and continued his search for Tom in the blue cap.

"Wait a minute," I said, plodding after him, unfolding the schedule. "Just wait a minute. Let's see now. Here. It stops at The Gulls. And it stops at Palm Ridge. That's where we ate the croissants yesterday. Now it's not that bloody far from the Refuge exit to Palm Ridge. At a good clip you could walk that in forty minutes easily. Then you hop on the trolley at Palm Ridge, ride down Tarpon Bay road and over to The Gulls, and you're all set. Or vice versa."

Greenfield stopped, studied the schedule, both routes, handed it back, walked on.

"You see," I insisted, "it could work. That's what Grafman did, I'm sure of it."

Greenfield spotted a blue cap near the path leading to the beach. He crossed the lawn in that direction. Tom looked up from under the shade of his blue bill, a pale face atop a sunburned neck and arms.

"Can you tell me," Greenfield asked, "if there's an oleander bush anywhere on this property?"

"No sir, no oleander. That stuff'll kill you. Chew a leaf or suck on a branch and you're finished. Looks pretty but I wouldn't have it around the place. Plenty of other shrubs you can use for landscaping. Nothing wrong with that hibiscus I've got over there, or the bougainvillea by the pool—"

Greenfield nodded, thanked him, we wandered down the path toward the beach.

"The library," he mused, "would probably have a picture of one."

"Or the MacIntosh bookstore. They have dozens of books on local flora. I saw them when I bought my *History of the Islands*.

Persky was—'' I stopped, puzzled. Greenfield waited patiently, eyebrows raised. ''—was there at the time,'' I went on slowly, ''looking at one of them.''

We made a little tableau there, on the edge of the beach, me stock-still, staring at Greenfield, Greenfield with his hands in his pockets and his bushy gray brows making furrows in his forehead, staring back.

After a while he turned and struck out over the sand and I followed.

All right, so Persky was looking at a book about local flora. Lots of people looked at those books. That's why they were there. Never mind the bloody book, what about the trolley schedule and Grafman? He hadn't commented on *that,* I noticed.

A few hardy souls, driven by the humid heat, were frolicking in the icy Gulf. Farther down the beach a large black bird sat at the edge of the water, its wings spread wide to dry. We walked in that direction, for no particular reason.

And then we were close enough to the water for me to see the black bird's wings. I stifled a cry and put out a hand to stop Greenfield.

''Look,'' I said quietly. ''I'd forgotten all about it. I meant to find one to show you. Look at the wings. Isn't it incredible? It's a *piano* bird.''

He looked. ''It's an anhinga,'' he said, unimpressed.

I turned on him, upset, annoyed, hot, frustrated. ''It may be an anhinga,'' I growled, ''but it *looks* like a *piano!*''

He stood looking at the bird. I walked on.

''You really have a talent,'' I said crossly, ''for deflating things. You take the *fun* out of them. Does it *matter* what the bloody *name* is? The marvelous thing is that it has a bloody *keyboard* on its wings. It's things like that—'' A woman coming toward me from the opposite direction looked at me strangely as she passed. I glanced over my shoulder. I was alone. Talking to myself. Greenfield was still back there, staring at the bird. I retraced my steps. ''Now what?'' I asked him, ''it's *not* an anhinga?''

He ran a hand through his hair. ''Tell me about the airport.''

''The *what*?''

"You said, originally, that you'd first seen Persky at the airport."

"That's right." I studied the anhinga for any resemblance to Persky. Apparently it was something only Greenfield could detect.

"What were the circumstances?"

"He was waiting for his bag to show up on the next carousel."

"And—?"

"And, I noticed him because he was having trouble finding his bag. He grabbed the first one, realized it wasn't his, put it back, waited, grabbed the next one, but that wasn't it either. You know how it is. When he checked the tag on the third one, he went off with it."

"What sort of bag?"

"One of those big canvas businesses. Green-and-blue plaid, as I remember."

"Plaid," he repeated softly. "And there were *three* of them going around?"

"Three. Yes."

"Three. Big. Plaid. Bags. Identical."

"No, of course not identical. One was a brown . . ."

To his credit, Greenfield didn't stay to watch the realization flood my face. He started back across the sand toward the Sea Grape, and after a moment I followed him, in abject confusion. Eventually he remarked, "If you'd been paying attention to that poolside conversation yesterday, it wouldn't come as a complete shock."

"I heard every word," I mumbled, "once I was out of the pool."

"Hearing is not necessarily synonymous with listening. Why do you think I engaged Persky in that banal discussion of Mahler last night?"

Wild horses wouldn't drag that answer out of me. "I thought you were being sociable," I lied.

"Maggie. Would you agree that you are—no derogation intended—a relatively small fish in the journalistic ocean?"

"A minnow," I agreed.

"Imagine you're Persky's age, with no ties. You're offered a post at the Paris bureau of the *Herald Tribune*, at a good salary.

A post which veteran reporters have been known to commit un-civilized acts to achieve. Would you, minnow though you are, hold out for twice the money offered? And when, against all likelihood, they agreed to that, would you press your luck even further and demand, in additon, a rent-free suite of rooms on the Rue Royale?''

"Only if I didn't want the job."

"You've capsulized it neatly."

I threw up my hands. "If he didn't want the job, why did he *come* here?''

"If you're really curious, you'll have to work quickly: he's scheduled to leave on the seven o'clock plane."

"Work at what?"

"Ransacking Persky's bag."

"His *bag*? How am I going to get my hands on his *bag*? It's in Grafman's apartment!''

"True. And unfortunately they don't deliver."

The piercing shriek of the maintenance crew hosing away at the back wall as we reached our building effectively silenced any comment I might have made. On the landing the maid service was leaving the Ruskin apartment, laden with the paraphernalia of housecleaning. In the cool but closed-up apart-ment, my mother was working at reading her Doris Lessing, and looking a little wilted. Greenfield told her we were going to need her assistance, and she came to life like a parched petunia that's finally been watered.

"I'm ready," she said, "but if it involves climbing a tree, I'll need help." God knows what she thought we were plan-ning.

"It's your voice we need. And your intelligence," he said.

"Both in pretty good shape."

"I'm already convinced of that." And having recruited her, he stood at the glass doors gazing at the listless palms, appar-ently without any concrete idea of what it was we were going to do. I couldn't imagine how I was to get into Grafman's apart-ment: it's all very well to decide you have to enter, uninvited, into a place that is locked with a key that you neither have nor can reasonably expect to acquire, but unless you happen to be on film, playing the part of a lovable veteran of the underworld who can pick locks with a piece of dental floss, the need is likely to remain unsatisfied.

I poured us each a glass of grapefruit juice, hoping the tartness would encourage constructive thoughts, but Greenfield came up with a possibility before he'd had even a swallow. He made a suggestion.

I looked up the office number at The Gulls, dialed it, and asked for Housekeeping, hoping fervently there wasn't already someone in C12 vacuuming away. In the voice of someone accustomed to receiving prompt service at Cartier's, I told Housekeeping I was C12 and needed maid service urgently. I was told I couldn't have anyone until eleven. Checking first with Greenfield, I agreed, but insisted that the girl be prompt because I was expecting company.

So much for that. But two primary obstacles had yet to be removed from that apartment, and I couldn't see how.

"On a day like this," I said, "only people who work in meat lockers will go outside voluntarily."

Greenfield dismissed my assessment. "You and I went out. Physical discomfort is easily endured under certain pressures. An overwhelming need, for instance. Or an overriding passion. I'm certain they have needs, but we don't know what they are. Their passions, on the other hand, are transparent." He coached my mother for several minutes and she picked up the phone.

We could hear it ringing, down at the Gold Coast cubes of The Gulls. It rang for a minute or so, to no response. We were beginning to eye each other in quiet uneasiness when the ringing was interrupted and a voice made an inquiring sound.

"This is the Hibiscus Gallery," the recruit said, as Elizabeth Barrett as she could get. "We have a painting here that was purchased by a Miss Thea Quinn. Who's this speaking, please? Mr. Grafman, we were terribly sorry to hear about Miss Quinn, and we don't quite know what to do about this painting. It's already been paid for, you see, and she left it here to be framed. A lovely watercolor, quite expensive, the artist is becoming well known and the painting is bound to increase in value. We thought you might want to pick it up. Today, yes. In fact, this morning. We're going to be closing for some repair work to be done on the building. No, I'm afraid that would be too late, could you make it by eleven?''

She gave him complicated directions (very good at that) to a point on Captiva that didn't exist, and replaced the receiver, trying to look modest about her bravura performance.

It was ten-thirty, or within a minute of it. Giving Grafman a ten-minute interval to depart, Greenfield called the number again.

Persky would not be there, I told myself, an immunization against failure. Why should he be there? He could be in an air-conditioned shop buying souvenirs to take home. He could be in an air-conditioned bar playing the video games. Why should he stay in the apartment?

He was in the apartment.

Greenfield concocted a fable about a grandson addicted to science fiction cinema, whose undying love could be obtained for the price of a few diagrams showing how certain effects had been obtained in his favorite movies. Could he, Greenfield, impose on Persky? He realized that time was short: in fact, he, Greenfield, would also be leaving the island, and in the next hour or so. And unfortunately he had no transport at the moment. But he would be happy to walk up the beach, if Persky could arrange to meet him roughly halfway. He could leave immediately and meet him, say, in fifteen minutes.

It won't work, I told myself. Why should anyone agree to walk on a hot beach to meet some gray-haired Mahler crank who wanted a favor? No matter how passionate about technology. It was a wild ploy, couldn't work.

It worked.

Greenfield nodded to me, I picked up the car keys and left. If I knew Greenfield, ''halfway'' meant Persky walking a mile toward the Sea Grape while Greenfield walked fifty feet toward The Gulls. Greenfield wouldn't be leaving for a while.

I made my way to the car, thinking *I am going to break and enter. I am going to poke into a stranger's personal belongings.*

And what did we have to go on? A book about plants, a plaid suitcase, a lie about Mahler.

It was strange. It was suspicious. It was, as Greenfield would say, *suggestive*. But aside, possibly, from the book, what did it have to do with Thea? I mopped my hot wet hands with a tissue.

The inside of the Ford could have competed successfully with the caldarium in any old Roman thermae. I debated leaving the windows shut to speed up the effectiveness of the air conditioner, but decided I would not reach the corner alive under those conditions. One window open, I dripped my way to Grafman's high-priced dormitory.

The blue Dodge was nowhere in evidence in The Gulls' parking area and I slipped into an empty slot and started along the outside corridor that led to the apartment. A girl with a cartful of towels, floor cleaner and scouring powder was knocking at the door to C12. I paused to see if anyone would come to the door: no one did, she used her key to let herself in. I reached the door before she could shut it from the inside.

"What's this?" I demanded.

"Maid service." She looked apprehensive.

"There's some mistake. We didn't call for maid service."

She took a slip of paper from her pocket. "C twelve."

"The housekeeper must have mistaken the number. We didn't call for cleaning help."

She hesitated, shrugged, moved her cart out to the corridor again, and I shut the door. And reset the lock. And turned the bolt. Though what good it would do me to be trapped inside if Housekeeping should decide to investigate? I couldn't imagine.

I stood in the living room for a moment, trying to slow down my galloping pulse, then moved down the hallway toward the back of the apartment. The two bedrooms were at right angles to each other; the large one (bed unmade, quilted lavender spread crumpled on a chair) I bypassed, the smaller one I entered. Two narrow single beds neatly spread with tan cotton covers, the dresser top bare except for a bottle of suntan lotion, a silvery token the size of a half-dollar that pictured the Sanibel trolley on one side, and the blue-covered manuscript Persky had been holding the day I'd returned. Thea's car keys. I pocketed the token and opened the blue binder.

Act I, Scene I. A palm tree and the dramatic outline of an eighteenth-century Spanish brigantine silhouetted against a night sky. Lights up. A horde of evil-looking pirates swarms down from the deck, drunk and laughing.

I riffled the pages. A small piece of paper fell to the floor. It had been torn from an address book, and the only words written on it, over and over again, were *Alvin Persky*. I slipped it into my bag, crossed to the louvered doors of the wardrobe and opened them. From the rack hung one white shirt and one pair of gray slacks. On the floor below them rested the blue-and-green-plaid suitcase.

Bottom lip between my teeth and pulse hammering in my throat, I lugged it to one of the beds and unzipped it.

Brightly colored sport shirts and cotton turtlenecks, an assortment of socks, underpants, several pairs of slacks, loafers and scuffs in plastic bags, eyeglasses in a case—I dropped those into my bag—a zippered case for toilet articles, empty except for a used toothbrush in a holder. In a snap-fastened pocket, a folder of traveler's checks, all of them signed "Alvin Persky" at the top, and a folded sheet of lined yellow paper. I unfolded it.

It was covered with stick-figure drawings, dots, arrows and cryptic notes running every which way across the page.

Program for single frame exp. n.g. BX code for D. and A. C has to oscillate. Optical printer? Hi cntrst drwng and synthesizer?

I added the yellow paper and one of the traveler's checks to the other articles I'd borrowed, removed a pair of slacks, shook them out, put them back, copied the address on the luggage tag in my notebook, zipped up the suitcase and replaced it on the floor of the wardrobe. What had he done with the book? I looked under the beds and found only dust balls. Maid service would not have been superfluous. I opened the dresser drawers, all of them empty. I looked in the large bedroom. *Variety* on the night table. A manuscript in a beige binder on the bed: *Potterbill's Luck*. The wardrobe doors were open, Thea's clothes hanging there, faintly scented. How did he bear it?

I went through the tiny kitchen and the living room. The *New York Times* lay in pieces on the floor, the *Wall Street Journal* on a chair. Not a book in the place. There was nothing left to do. I was done, with time to spare.

I spared a moment of it in compassion for Greenfield, sweltering out there, learning how to make science fiction magic.

A last look around, then I unbolted the front door, opened it, caught my breath and shut it again. That figure approaching the building was Persky! How could that be? I looked wildly around the room, as though the furniture might offer sanctuary. What the *hell* had happened? Where was Greenfield? Had he been struck down by the heat on the beach? Had Persky somehow suspected something and done him harm? Was Greenfield floating out in the Gulf?

Paralyzed with the disaster of imminent discovery, I could do nothing but stand there clutching my incriminating shoulder bag. I heard footsteps approaching from the far end of the corridor. *Outside,* was all I could think. *I have to get outside.* The only exit available was the one to the balcony. I spurted across the room, undid the catch on the sliding glass doors with fingers like bananas, slid it open eight inches and it stuck! I struggled with it for precious seconds, then squeezed agonizingly through the opening and stood there, outside at last.

In full view, through the glass doors, of anyone entering the apartment.

I looked over the railing. Not more than a ten-foot drop. Grass was softer than cement. Suppose someone saw me? Games. I was playing games. I hoisted myself up onto the railing, swung my legs over and dropped into bush, with a crash of twigs. Just my luck, I thought, scrambling to my feet, it'll be an oleander and it pierced the skin.

I grinned for a possible audience, waved gaily at the balcony, and limped away as quickly as the shock to my bones would allow, wishing I could run, though I knew running was the last thing to do after committing a crime. Back to the far end of the building, around to the parking area, into the Ford, quivering with tension. For a quarter of a mile I was a menace on that road. Blind and deaf, my foot pushing the accelerator through the floorboard to the claypan below the island, I was a streak of concentrated adrenaline in flight. The consequences of being discovered by Persky in that apartment shook me as though they were actually occurring. Persky. Or whatever his name was. An anhinga, passing himself off as a piano.

What had he done with Greenfield?

Or hadn't he met him? Had he gone halfway and, not seeing him, turned back? Or had Greenfield after all left the apartment immediately, and had Persky outsmarted him, waited at the other end for Greenfield to do all the walking? It was much too hot to walk that distance. Mad dogs and Englishmen. Greenfield had collapsed. I could see it. People gathering around the man lying unconscious in the sand. Ambulance called for. No one would know who he was. Rushed to the hospital in Fort Myers. By helicopter.

The traffic on Periwinkle seemed to have multiplied a hundredfold. It crawled from one end to the other like a disoriented centipede.

Where was *Greenfield*!

Persky had tumbled to the clumsy ruse, sensed that something was up. A guilty man is wary, suspicious, out of self-defense. First Grafman is lured away, and then this patently absurd request to meet on the beach: someone is on to him. Greenfield is dangerous. Dispose of him. Wait him out. Walk him into some shrubbery. Strangle him. Who knows what this piano bird is capable of doing. My God. Greenfield.

There, finally, was the Sea Grape up ahead!

And there, lounging at the entrance to the parking area, gazing nonchalantly down the road, was Greenfield. I zoomed into a parking space.

"Where *were* you!" I hissed furiously as he sauntered over. "Do you realize what *happened*? Do you realize he came back to the apartment *while I was still there*? Do you know he almost *caught* me? I had to jump off the bloody *balcony*? I could have broken my *back*? I fell into a bush that probably *poisoned* me? What did you do, change your mind at the last *minute*? Decide Persky wasn't worth *bothering* about? Or that it was too *hot* for a walk on the beach? Figured I'd work my way out of it *somehow*?"

He strolled away from me and went to the foot of the outside stairway. The maintenance men with their aqueous artillery were now blasting the building next to ours. Greenfield pointed eloquently to the shrieking jets of water.

"I was about to leave," he said loudly, "when they trained those on your mother's front door!"

I stared at what was coming out of the hoses: Niagara-gone-horizontal-and-vicious. An enemy barrage, screaming and impenetrable. A tidal wave of water and possibly Mr. Clean, that could conceivably, with that force, remove human skin.

Timing is everything.

CHAPTER SIXTEEN

IN THE APARTMENT, MY MOTHER LOOKED PALE AND shaken, and squeezed my hand until my ring embedded itself permanently in my finger. I was not to be appeased. Riding high on the aftermath of panic.

"Why," I demanded, "didn't you ask them to *stop*, so you could get *out*?"

Greenfield gave me a withering look. "I thought of that. I thought of opening the door to ask them. But there would have been so much mopping up to do."

"I mean the *office*! Why didn't you call the *office* and tell them to *stop* it for a minute!"

"We tried," Mother contributed. "We couldn't get through. The switchboard was tied up."

"Why didn't you call *me*? There's a *phone* at Grafman's!"

"Would you," Greenfield asked with deadly calm, "have answered the ring?"

No. Of couse not. Pick up Grafman's phone and say hello while I was rifling his guest's luggage? What am I, witless? I redirected my hysteria. "You'd think they'd *alert* the tenants before barring their only exit from the apartment!"

"They did." The tenant in question averted her eyes. "They came around while the two of you were on the beach, and said they'd be blocking the doorway shortly. But in all the excitement . . ."—she trailed off—"The phone calls and so on . . ." Then, with a logic only another mother could understand, "It would have served me right if anything had happened to you."

I fell onto the sofa and closed my eyes.

Greenfield was sprawled in the easy chair, as though he'd recently been through unparalleled torture and had no time for anyone else's traumas. "I assume," he murmured, "that in your own good time, you'll let me know whether or not you found anything."

Without moving, I reached into my bag and handed him the two slips of paper, the single traveler's check, the notebook with luggage-tag address, and the case containing the eyeglasses. Reaching into my pocket, I tossed him the trolley token. He examined them all, put on the glasses, took them off, and looked at me questioningly.

"He identified a plover on the beach all the way from Grafman's balcony, without glasses. At the airport he read that luggage tag without glasses. If there's anything better than twenty-twenty vision, that's probably what he has."

A glance from Mother, lying flat on the floor with her head on a cushion: an ophthalmologist's daughter knows there's nothing better.

"I held a pair of slacks from the suitcase up against me," I added. "They just about reached my ankles. They'd make this man look like a twelve-year-old who's suddenly shot up. I thought he was addicted to gray slacks and owned five pairs of them, but evidently he was wearing the same ones all the time. Until last night."

"Until he perfected his penmanship," Greenfield said, looking at the traveler's check and the slip of paper covered with *Alvin Perskys*.

"He was broke."

"Or had limited funds."

"And no luggage of his own."

Greenfield stared at the opposite wall and pushed his chin up into his lower lip.

"He got rid of the plant book," I said. "It wasn't anywhere in the apartment."

He nodded.

"So tell me, Charlie. Why did he come here?" No answer. "To pick up a suitcase?"

"Possibly."

"Why?"

Greenfield sighed. "I have nothing against conjecture, it was conjecture that led to the invention of the wheel. But at this stage it's irrelevant."

"Why irrelevant? We're assuming he killed Thea. *Why* is not irrelevant. If *why* he came here leads to *why* he killed her, and that's not relevant, then what, for God's sake, is relevant?"

"*How* is relevant." He stood up impatiently. "Without a car, without a boat, without a bicycle or a moped, without the necessary physical condition to run that number of miles in the alloted time—*how* did he get to the Refuge and back?"

I picked up the trolley token from the coffee table, shook it at him, let it drop with a clatter onto the table. He went to the balcony doors and looked out.

"Why not?" I demanded. "Where's the map?" I found the map, dug the trolley schedule out of my bag. "Charlie, look. Look, will you!" He turned and looked. "Thea and I separated about a quarter to three. She was only minutes away from the Gasparilla trail and walking toward it. Even allowing a half-hour for him to get her to where he left her, he could have been on his way home by a quarter past and down at Palm Ridge by four o'clock. Look—here's the Refuge exit, stone's throw from the trail, right? Here's Palm Ridge. He gets there by four, the trolley"—I pointed to the schedule—"doesn't reach Palm Ridge for another ten minutes, and then it just carries him down Tarpon Bay road and over to The Gulls by four-twenty-one, I walk in at four-thirty, and there he is!"

Greenfield turned away.

"Well? What's wrong with that?"

"The girl," he said, "left the restaurant, in the car, with Grafman and Persky, at ten minutes before two. There was no possibility of their reaching The Gulls by two o'clock, with time for both Grafman and the girl to be on their separate ways, leaving Persky free to board the trolley that stops there at two-oh-one. I grant you he could make it *back* from the Refuge. Now you tell me how he managed to follow that girl *to* the Refuge, in time to get her out of sight before she succumbed."

Slowly I lowered my head to a sofa cushion, curled into a fetal ball and withdrew from the world.

"Yes, well," I said wearily, "I have but one life to give for my country and I've used it up."

Greenfield looked out at the darkening sky. Smoky purple, I thought, was not a promising color for midday. There must be tons of water up there waiting to descend.

The silence was broken by my mother, from the floor.

"Maybe he went *with* her," she said.

Nobody moved or spoke for quite a while.

Finally, I said, "I *asked* her if anyone was with her. She said no. Why would she say that? And why didn't she get him to help with the locked door? And if he was there, where was he? He wasn't in the car, obviously, because—"

The seconds ticked by.

In measured tones, without turning, Greenfield said, "Finish the thought, or your leap from Grafman's balcony will have been the pleasurable high point of your day."

"No. It's impossible."

"Maggie."

"All right. Thea dropped Persky and Grafman at The Gulls, Grafman got out of the car and went . . . somewhere. Back to the room. Persky got out of the car and just . . . stayed there. Hung around. The trolley had to have come and gone by then, so he couldn't take the trolley. But *Thea* . . . didn't just take off for the Refuge immediately. She went back to the room first. Leaving the car alone."

"That's a large supposition."

"Not so large, because later . . . at the Refuge, when she found the car locked, she said, 'If it had to happen, why couldn't it have happened *before*, when I went back to the room, where the spare keys are!' "

Greenfield was still turned away, but I could tell from his utter stillness that if he'd been a dog, his ears would have been pricked up.

"So . . ." I went on, "she went back to the room, with Grafman, to pick up something, binoculars or who knows what, or maybe to use the john and Persky stayed outside, near the car. *And* . . . now you *said* you have nothing against conjecture . . ." I took a deep breath of air conditioning. "There was a rug in the backseat of Thea's car. On the floor, all rumpled. A big, woven, striped thing, maybe eight feet of it, the kind of thing you'd use to sit on, for a picnic."

Greenfield still hadn't moved. He remained at the glass doors looking out at the ominous, bruise-colored sky. He might have been a piece of peculiar Roman statuary, chiseled in something from a Carrara quarry.

"He waited until there was no one around, until she was on her way up to the observation tower," I suggested, "then he locked the car doors behind him before sneaking out of the car. They weren't far from the Gasparilla trail and the exit. He couldn't take the chance that she'd come back and drive right out of the Refuge without stopping again. He wanted her stranded, so that he could make his move. He was hiding in the bushes when I drove up. He must have been in a panic until we separated."

No response from the statue.

"What do you think?" I prodded. "Is it possible?"

"He couldn't have counted on her going back to the room," he said. "But he might have counted on the trolley, and been forced to improvise."

He looked at his watch. "It'll have to do. I think someone in a uniform should ask the man with Persky's bag a few pertinent questions. Before he becomes unavailable."

Our hostess rolled onto all fours, labored to her feet with

the assistance of the sofa, waving me away, and said, "Tuna salad? Iced tea? Bakery rolls?"

Greenfield moved. "Do you have a shoe box?" he asked her.

"For *lunch*?"

As it was my mother who asked, Greenfield merely lowered his eyes and repeated, "Do you?"

"Several," she said.

"Is there a hardware store nearby?"

"Bailey's has everything."

He looked at me. "Let's go."

"Now?"

But he was at the door.

Captive in the passenger seat, he was obliged to answer when I asked about his shopping list, but he did it obliquely. "The plane to Miami that connects with a flight to Los Angeles leaves Fort Myers at seven o'clock. Our man may or may not be headed for Los Angeles, but that's his story, and to back it up he would reasonably leave the island anytime between five and six."

"And whatever you're buying at Bailey's," I nodded, "is designed to keep him on the island. Six pounds of drugged cough drops. Wrapped in a shoe box."

But what he bought was solder and a soldering iron, pliers, a lantern battery, four automobile flares, a cheap wristwatch, a length of electrical wire, a large manila envelope, wire cutters and pliers, a tube of glue and a roll of electrician's tape.

"My mother," I said, eyeing his shopping bag warily as we drove back, "is very fond of her apartment. She likes the walls where they are."

Greenfield peered at the threatening sky. "It doesn't take professional expertise to assemble these things without altering the shape of the building."

"No? Your average person in the street would know what to do with that grab bag? *I* wouldn't."

"*I* couldn't knit a bootee," he said, "but neither activity requires a summa cum laude."

I was not reassured. When he took the shopping bag, the I. Miller shoe box he got from my mother, a few sheets of old newspaper and a glass of iced tea into his bedroom and shut the door, Mother and I pecked at our tuna-salad, listening uneasily to the muted scratchings, rustlings and snippings.

At three-thirty he asked for scissors, a sheet of writing paper and an envelope, and handed them to me, with instructions. I had barely finished the job when he emerged from his room, manilá envelope in one had, shoe box under his arm.

"If you're going to do *this*"—I held up my envelope— "why do you need *that*?" I indicated the shoe box.

"Do *you* guarantee the police will act on that letter?"

Ten minutes later, with great kettledrums of thunder overhead, we were driving along the causeway road in the direction of San Carlos Bay. Greenfield looked at the swollen, lowering darkness above us.

"The dead of night would have been preferable," he said, "but this at least should discourage the sightseers and amateur fishermen."

I hoped so, but you can never tell with people who fish.

At the beginning of the causeway the verge descended in a gentle slope to a narrow shelf of land buttressed by a retaining wall that rose no higher than ground level. No protection to speak of: backing up to take a picture was a certain prelude to a dunking in the bay. It was here that Greenfield wanted to stop, and fortunately no one else had decided to do the same; the stretch of grass at the top of the slope was clear of human traffic.

I pulled off the road and he got out of the car and came around to the driver's side. "If some idiot decides to stop and pick wildflowers, lean on the horn."

I nodded, took the shoe box from the seat beside me, slid it out the window to him, away from the casually prying eye of any passing motorist, and he disappeared down the slope. It was seventeen minutes past four.

I sat there watching the yellow lights of cars approaching the island from the far side of the causeway, the red lights of traffic going in the opposite direction. I willed them to go on by, not to stop, not even to pause. The nose of the Ford was pointing at the bay. As a precaution I got out, opened the trunk and stood the folding beach chair up aginst the bumper. Would it be less likely to arouse undue interest if I released the hood of the car and stood peering at its insides as though the car had malfunctioned? Or would that only attract the automotive Galahads? On the other hand, a woman sitting alone in a car for no apparent reason, with a thunderstorm looming, might be an invitation in itself, and would certainly be remembered in the light of subsequent events.

In the end I left the car and stood at the top of the slope, looking down at the bay: an innocent tourist taking in the scenery. I even waved, occasionally, to an imaginary companion. Becoming quite a performer, Maggie.

From there I could see that the ledge below curved eventually to meet the underpinnings of the causeway: massive concrete stanchions shouldering the road above at intervals all across the bay.

(Prestressed concrete. Was Elliot even now down at the site with the Peruvian engineers, explaining the changes in the stress allowance? Down on some arid, dusty shore where no greenery grew among the sand-logged rocks? No terrorists around there, he had said. How could he be sure?)

I searched among the stanchions for a sight of Greenfield's buff-colored shirt, and saw nothing.

I wondered what the penalty was for what we were doing. I thought about the man to whom we were doing it. What went on behind that boyish face, that polite smile? Where had he been, in his young life, what did he want so desperately? And if he had, really, taken Thea over that Indian mound and left her to die—an ambiguous death, which, with luck, would be interpreted as accidental—for what reason? What on earth, or in space, or wherever, had he and Persky been up to? And where, come to think of it, was—

Behind me a car pulled off the road. I whirled around. A navy-blue Pontiac with a dented rear fender. The passenger door opened and a thin, harried woman got out, brushing lank brown hair from her cheek. She opened a rear door and a small boy of six or seven came whimpering out. She took his hand impatiently, spoke in a low, frazzled voice. "Why didn't you *say* something before we *left*!" Dragging him toward some bushes.

"I din' *know*."

"What do you mean you didn't know? How could you not know?"

"I din' *hafta*."

"All right, come on."

"Noooo! Not here."

"Yes, here. It's all right."

"Everybody c'n *see*!"

"Nobody can see. Come on, now—"

I had turned away almost immediately and taken cover at the front of the Ford. I thought about sounding the horn, but after a quick look at the weary man behind the wheel, turned in his seat to lock the back door against two more bobbing children's heads, I decided to wait it out.

They were headed off-island, with Georgia license plates, all to the good, but I was glad I'd placed my mother's folding beach chair up against the rear plates of the Ford. I kept my face averted and scanned the ledge below, poised to signal Greenfield if he appeared. He didn't. Behind me I could hear the young mother exhorting her son to be absolutely sure he was finished. Then the slam of a car door, pause, another slam, grind of starting motor, and they were gone.

It was four-thirty-five. Come on, Charlie, hurry it up.

I felt raindrops on my hair and looked up. Far down the bay there seemed to be a curtain of rain suspended between sky and water, and as I watched, it moved toward the causeway.

Bloody hell, I thought, and got into the car.

At four-thirty-nine, simultaneously, the deluge broke above me and Greenfield appeared, scrambling up the slope.

He got into the car, wiping water from his face with the back of his hand.

"Will you be able to drive in this?" he asked.

I looked at the torrent sluicing down the windshield. "I'll be able to drive. What I won't be able to do is *see*."

"We can't stay here."

"It's all right," I said gamely. "I can find my way back by the bread crumbs."

With infinite care I backed and turned, and drove back down the causeway road toward Periwinkle.

"We need a public telephone. Not too public."

"A little radar wouldn't hurt either," I followed two little glimmers of light ahead of me in the downpour. "You don't suppose this could develop into a hurricane?"

Greenfield laughed. Actually laughed. At least I interpreted the sound as such.

"You have a macabre sense of humor."

"Maggie. Think about it. An order to evacuate the island. And I've just gone to infinite pains to cut off the only exit. It would be the ultimate hoisting of a man by his own petard."

"Yes, well, I'll be happy to forgo the delicious irony." I turned carefully onto Periwinkle. Already there were small lakes at intervals along the road. "The only complete phone booth I've seen is in front of Bailey's, and you'd better have a booth, you can't use one of those uncovered phones, you'll drown before you dial the last digit."

But as we reached Bailey's parking lot, the rain stopped, an abrupt and unnatural cessation that brought no relief, only the feeling that something worse was going to happen. Greenfield slogged to the phone in his wet clothes and I tagged along, my presence required, he said, to run interference in the event that someone ventured close enough to hear what was being said. Needless to say, he was not going to lock himself into a phone booth without air.

Not only was someone close, she was using the phone, with the air of one who has taken up residence. Run into the booth when the storm broke, no doubt, and just stayed there, calling everyone she knew.

"Martha? Oh, who's this? Lois! Hi, honey, when'd you get home? Uh-huh. Uh-huh. And how was it? You don't say. Yeah, I heard, twenty inches of snow. You don't say.

Really. Well, I'll bet you're glad you don't live there. And how's your brother doing up there? You don't say." She, also, had the door open. Another claustrophobe.

Greenfield looked at his watch. "There must be another telephone in the area."

"There is, but I don't remember where. Shall I ask and draw attention to myself?"

It was not a question that required a reply. By the same token it wouldn't have done to pluck at her sleeve and plead an emergency, nor to yell "Fire!"

"Martha? No, I'm still on the island . . ."

It was four-fifty-two. Granted, five o'clock was an arbitrary deadline, but it was as logical as arbitrary can get, and certainly preferable to five-twenty or even five-fifteen.

At seven minutes before five the woman departed. There was no one else within earshot. Greenfield deposited the coin and dialed Grafman's number while I flipped through the telephone book. I could hear the phone ringing at the other end: three times, four, six, nine. Finally Greenfield replaced the receiver, immediately deposited another coin and said grimly, "He's gone."

Had Grafman, at least, been there, we'd know how long ago the man had left, and could, if necessary, call the whole thing off. As it was . . . Greenfield dialed the number I indicated in the phone book. He made his short, anonymous speech to police headquarters, alerting them to the crime he'd just committed, and we returned to the car.

I said, "I figure three years at hard labor, what do you figure?"

"They have to suspect me first. And then they have to prove it."

We got into the car. Greenfield looked extremely downcast. I tried for optimism. "He probably walked out the door while you were dialing. It would take him easily fifteen minutes to get to the causeway. Especially if he started out in the storm. He's probably not there yet. There's still a chance."

His expression didn't lighten by so much as a whit. He picked up the manila envelope. "This has to be returned."

He picked up the smaller envelope containing the newsprint message I'd put together. "This has to be delivered. The police first."

As he said it, a brown-and-tan police car came streaking around the bend from the San–Cap road, siren wailing, speeding toward the causeway.

"Faster!" I breathed, and pulled out of the parking lot.

The message I had taped together from words and letters I'd snipped out of the newspaper lacked imagination, originality, lyricism, wit, and was visually anything but an aesthetic triumph. However, it did convey the necessary warning: "GraFmAn hOuSe gueST posING as PERsky passING forGEd T-cheCkS."

The trick would be to get it into the proper hands.

"You have any suggestions," I asked, "as to how we can arrange to be invisible while delivering this message?"

"According to Boccaccio, if you could get your hands on a green stone called heliotrope, that would do it."

"Does it cover two people?"

"I don't intend to be anywhere near the place. You can drop me at the arcade across the road."

"Lovely." All I needed was to be identified by that sharp-eyed policewoman at the switchboard as having been in the vicinity on some pretext immediately after an anonymous phone call and just before the discovery of an anonymous letter.

I stopped at the arcade and Greenfield got out and under shelter and began to stroll past the shop windows. I looked across the San–Cap road at the building that housed police headquarters, visualizing the stairway ascending to the second floor, the glassless window that gave onto the switchboard, a door to the left of the window, opening off the landing. No place to hide. If I did nothing but open the street door and place the envelope on the stairs, some police officer could decide to go up or down those stairs at that moment. The same held true for sneaking up the stairs on all fours and shoving the letter under the door, or onto the ledge of the window.

There was a police cruiser parked to one side of the building. I could slip the letter under the windshield wipers, if I wanted everyone within two hundred feet to notice me. Plenty of people around for that: the attendants at the pumps of the filling station in front of the building, the people going into the general store next to the City Council Chamber, people in cars, waiting to have their gas tanks filled. . . .

There were three cars waiting there.

I left the Ford where it was, went into the drugstore and bought a roll of double-stick tape. Back in the car, I attached a length of tape to the envelope on the front of which were taped the newsprint letters URGENT—POLICE, stuck it to my shoulder bag, held that side of the bag against me, and ran across the road. By that time the first of the three waiting cars had moved up to the pump, leaving two cars waiting. The second of these, its rear end at the extreme outer edge of the station area, was a two-tone Plymouth. Keeping the bag against me, I separated letter and tape from bag, and as I skirted the back end of the Plymouth, slapped them onto the car directly above the fuel-tank nozzle.

Without breaking stride, I continued on to the City Council Chamber and slipped inside, my pulse outstripping the speed of the police car heading for the causeway. Had they made it in time? Was he still on the island?

There was a meeting in progress, so well attended that several people were standing behind the rows of occupied chairs, their backs to the entrance. I mingled, unobtrusively. At the far end of the room the council members sat at a table facing the chairs, one of them addressing a man who had risen from his chair near a large wall map illustrating development density in the various sections of the island. Whatever was being said was largely an unintelligible drone: acoustically the room was not quite concert-hall caliber. I heard the word "problem" several times: "Procedural problem," "Agenda problem." And "concerned citizen" and "adjacent neighbor" came through loud and clear.

Adjacent neighbors, I thought, were certainly a problem on this island, and a citizen concerned about high-density development was the reason I was hiding here waiting for someone to discover an anonymous note. I longed to leave, without being conspicuous, to see what was happening out by the gas pumps. When a man in the back row stood up and made for the door, I went with him, contriving to look, as we emerged, as though we were together.

The car in front of the Plymouth was about to be serviced. Another police cruiser had parked behind the first, and two officers were hurrying toward it from the building. As I followed the man from the meeting across the service area they piled into the police car and took off, not exactly dawdling. Greenfield turns a somnolent isle into Forty-second Street.

I ran back across the road to where the Ford was standing. Greenfield sat in the passenger seat reading a copy of the *Islander*.

"Watch," I said, sliding behind the wheel and pointing across the road to where the Plymouth was moving up to the pump.

The attendant leaned down to the driver's window, nodded, detached a hose and went to the back of the car. He reached one hand to the nozzle of the gas tank, and froze. Then, slowly, he attached the hose, tore the envelope from the car, went back to the driver's window and displayed the envelope. The driver, apparently, denied ownership. The attendant then showed it to the other attendant, who grinned and said something. The first attendant ran, envelope in hand, across the service area, around the side of the building and in through the door to police headquarters.

I turned to Greenfield, anticipating at the very least an expression of restrained awe.

It was *very* restrained. "Unfortunately," he said, "Mr. Pulitzer never anticipated the need for recognizing achievement in skulduggery."

Covert praise was a Greenfield speciallty.

I started the car and drove away toward The Gulls, the manila envelope marked FOR C12, containing Persky's eyeglasses and traveler's check, the paper covered with copies of his signature and the one covered with diagrams and notes, was deposited, unnoticed, on the counter in The Gulls' busy office. We returned to the Sea Grape in silence, our thoughts, I was certain, identical: had the man with Persky's bag been stopped in time?

Or had he made it off the island?

We'd barely changed into dry clothes when a small tattoo on the apartment door heralded the arrival of my mother's birdlike friend with the red hair. In she came, enveloped in transparent lavender plastic rain gear.

"Have you heard? They've closed down the causeway! Somebody planted two *bombs* under it! They found one and they're still looking for the other! Bombs! On Sanibel!"

My mother didn't bat an eyelash. "Maybe they'll start up the ferry again," she said.

When her friend was gone Mother turned to Greenfield. *"Two?"*

"Some eager cop was bound to spot the shoe box in the first ten minutes. It was hardly worth closing down the causeway for that."

My mother gave him a hard look. "How dangerous *was* that shoe box?"

He shrugged. "It's possible that in trying to untape it from the pillar a man could break a fingernail."

CHAPTER SEVENTEEN

THE MAN WITH PERSKY'S BAG HAD MADE IT OFF THE IS-land before the causeway was closed. And disappeared.

Despite all his cautionary words about Galileo, Napoleon and Da Vinci, it was a failure that stuck in Greenfield's craw and gave him—and me—no peace.

I could have accepted it. We'd done our best. The Sanibel police, we learned, had followed through on our newsprint message. They'd questioned Grafman and secured from him the manila envelope containing the eyeglasses, traveler's check and bits of paper, together with a newsprint note Greenfield had included that identified the objects as contents of Persky's suitcase. They'd called Persky's Los Angeles agent, who eventually confirmed that Persky seemed to have vanished, and they'd communicated with the Los Angeles P.D. Most of all, from my viewpoint, we'd solved the problem of what had to be done about Sarah McChesney: namely, nothing.

Greenfield, however, brooded. That he had been within a hair's-breadth of netting a killer only to lose him at the last minute was not something he could banish from his mind. He was testy. He was restive. The subject was like a bruised elbow with a fatal attraction for every doorjamb and table corner. I had to be careful to avoid words like "bomb" or "bridge" or "Los Angeles." He could not let it go. If he'd had the resources he would have launched a worldwide manhunt.

But he had no such resources, and it was some time before the man who posed as Persky was found, and tried.

Not, as it turned out, for Thea's murder. It was another discovery and another deduction that led, eventually, to his trial. It began with Elliot's return.

He came back from Peru on a cold, slushy night, the streets full of used snow that had turned to icy brown mush during the day and was now frozen into myriad perilous ridges affording no safe purchase to boots, rubbers or galoshes. A nice welcome home. He called from Miami, where all good little planes from Lima must stop for customs and where his had arrived with engine trouble. There would be an indefinite delay in his departure for New York, he said, and I was in no condition to try to meet his flight, whenever that might be—he'd take an expense-paid cab.

It was a Wednesday, and on Wednesdays by long-standing tradition, having put the *Reporter* to bed for that week, Greenfield and I dined at the same table: mine. This Wednesday Greenfield had declined, his sense of fitness prohibiting his intrusion into a marital reunion. I called to tell him the reunion had been postponed, and so, a few minutes past seven, he clomped up the salt-strewn path to my front door and came in from the cold, his tan suede loafers in his hand, a pair of ferocious-looking steel-studded boots on his feet, and a look on his face of transcendent disgust.

"There's no question," he said, as though we'd been debating the point in the previous minute, "the man had to use one of those traveler's checks to pay for his plane ticket. They shouldn't have to do more than punch a few buttons to find out which plane he took and where it was going." He unbuttoned his heavy duffel coat. "Why can't they do that? This is the era of escalating sophistication. There's enough sophisticated technology floating around this country to determine who, at this moment, is having a tooth pulled in Harare, Zimbabwe. We have sophisticated banking, sophisticated genetics, sophisticated kindergartens—" He removed his spiked boots. "Even the old *horrors* are no longer sophisticated enough for us. 'Man's inhumanity to man' will soon be an obsolete phrase. We've come up with the more sophisticated concept that mankind *in toto* is dispensable." He prowled into the living room. "We can now achieve everything monstrous or irrelevant with the speed of light. Apparently the sole endeavor that has successfully resisted acceleration is the tracking down of an escaped criminal."

"Charlie," I said, "I don't want to hear about it."

I quickly poured bourbon into a glass and handed it to him, while George, with a red setter's doggedness, sat on one of Greenfield's feet waiting to have his ears scratched. "It's a lost cause. Forget it. We're going to listen to music." I was a little testy myself: I didn't care for the idea of Elliot flying in a plane with engine trouble. I took a tape of Handel's *Water Music* from the very large stack I'd lined up, and put it in the machine. This was the first opportunity there'd been for a little musical gluttony since our return from the island and the starvation diet of what Greenfield referred to as the Boston Pops Retrospective.

While the spinach salad and the veal piccata disappeared, and the dishes didn't get done, I kept both of us distracted with Brahms, Mahler, Scarlatti, Borodin, Walton, Satie, Rachmaninoff and Castelnuovo-Tedesco. With the second cup of coffee I put on the Beethoven Seventh, a recording I'd bought in all innocence. Greenfield glowered.

"Von Karajan rips through that," he said, "as though he were late for an appointment at Berchtesgaden."

As I started for the kitchen to stack the dishes, Elliot arrived. George went berserk with joy.

"This day," Elliot said, fending him off, "has been two weeks long," and greeted me with a weary kiss.

Greenfield stood up and came to the door, bent on tact. "I'm relieved to see you're back safely, Elliot. Some time in the near future I'd like to hear what's really going on down there." He reached for his boots.

"You must have been in Miami for hours," I sympathized.

"Three," Elliot said. "And it was hot. A few of us rented a car and drove down to the bay to cool off and look at the ships. It was better than hanging around the airport." He put his coat on a hanger. Greenfield took *his* coat off one. "Actually, there was a little excitement at the bay. In a grisly sort of way. The place was crawling with police. Coast guard boats were coming and going—"

Greenfield took his gloves from a pocket and opened the door an inch as a prelude to leaving.

Elliot picked up his bag. "Somebody said they found the body of a man washed up on one of the Bay islands. Drowned, it seems."

Greenfield shut the door. "Did they know who he was?"

"I don't think so. I heard a cop say, 'No identification.' " He yawned. "Other than that, and Aero Peru's stuttering engine, it was a long, dull trip."

"Are you hungry?" I asked.

"God, no. I've been eating junk all day."

"Was he a *young* man?" Greenfield asked.

Elliot looked at him. "I don't know. Why?"

"Just curious." Greenfield opened the door again, and this time said good-night, and left.

"I wish you hadn't mentioned that episode while he was here," I said, following Elliot and his bag to the bedroom. The only question in my mind was what *precisely* Greenfield would try to do with the information.

What he did was to call during breakfast and ask for Elliot, who was on his way out.

"He's going to the office," I said. "He has to catch a train."

"Ask him how long it took him to get from Miami airport to the bay."

I winced and asked. "Twenty minutes or so."

"Mm. I'm going to the city. I'll be back sometime this afternoon."

"The *city*? What do you mean, 'the city'? Why the city?"

"When you finish the report on the Gorham Road landfill, put it on my desk."

"Charlie? What are you going to do?"

The line was dead. I dressed at top speed, picked my way carefully down the front walk to the Honda, drove out to Poplar Avenue and down Poplar to the old white mansard-roofed house where Greenfield's Plymouth was already backing down the drive from the garage at the rear.

He stopped as I got out of the car and minced across the ice in my spikeless boots.

"That footwear is an invitation to disaster," he said.

"Where are you going?"

"To see Grafman."

"*Grafman*! *Why*? What are you—? Not without *me*!"

There was a short exchange of conflicting points of view, but I prevailed, locked my car, got in beside him, and we drove south to the city, at Greenfield's relentless forty miles an hour, while vintage rattletraps tore past us, sounding horns.

He'd made an appointment to see Grafman, who was back in New York conducting business. Why? Because, Greenfield said, Persky couldn't swim.

"There were no swim trunks in that suitcase," he said. "I find it unbelievable that the average young man would pack for a stay at a beach without including swimming gear, unless he couldn't swim. And the man who had the suitcase was careful to include that in his impersonation. If you remember that first conversation on the beach with Grafman, Webber, the girl and our man."

I could hear Webber's voice: *You don't have to know how to swim to go in a boat around the island.*

"So?"

But he was driving, and that demanded concentration. I was forced to wait until we'd traversed Fifty-seventh Street—in itself an experience, with Greenfield stoically ignoring New York taxicabs—parked in a vertical lot, and found Grafman's office in an elderly brick building on Seventh Avenue.

A ravishingly beautiful black girl sat at a cluttered desk in the small, dusty outer office, more of a foyer than a room, the walls plastered with framed posters of past productions, photographs of actors and actresses, theater marquees, scenes from plays. She was speaking into a phone and the moment she replaced the receiver the phone rang again. A door at the far end of the space was half open and Mitchell Grafman's rasp could be heard alternating with a high pitched nasal female voice, the owner of which eventually emerged wearing a heavy purple cape, dyed black hair and green eye makeup and carrying a sheaf of legal-looking papers.

We finally gained entrance to Grafman's sanctum, large and

with windows overlooking the avenue, but equally dusty, photograph-plastered, with a worn green carpet and a tantalizing odor from the delicatessen below. Grafman, in pale-blue cashmere turtleneck and tweed jacket, greeted us aggressively with ''What's going on?'' I found him as abrasive as ever.

Greenfield made himself comfortable in the only armchair, informed Grafman that what he had to say was urgent and requested that Grafman tell the secretary to hold all calls.

''What is this?'' Grafman lit a cigarillo impatiently. ''You said it was about Thea. What do you know about Thea? Who are you, anyway? You're no investor, right? What, then, some kind of detective? I *thought* there was something phony about you. And that business with Persky's suitcase—was it you who got hold of that stuff? What's your—''

When Grafman ran out of questions, Greenfield said quietly, ''I'm here to give you a hypothesis that may possibly lead to the prosecution of Miss Quinn's killer. If you're interested, you'll have to give me your assurance that my name and Mrs. Rome's will be kept out of anything you pass on to the police. In the pursuit of information we've both done things that are outside the law, otherwise I'd have taken this to the police myself. As it is, you can offer them this as your own theory, and they're bound to listen, given that you're vitally involved.''

''Why? Why should you have a theory? How did you get into all this?''

Greenfield explained. Grafman listened.

''And I'm here now,'' Greenfield said, ''because a body has been washed up on an island in Biscayne Bay.''

''And you think it's the guy who said he was Persky.''

''No, Mr. Grafman. I think it's Persky. The real Persky. And I think the man you knew as Persky put him there.''

Grafman raised his eyebrows in a grimace of skepticism.

Greenfield ignored it. ''They both came,'' he went on, ''from Los Angeles. There's no direct flight from Los Angeles to Fort Myers. This Persky—the real Persky, the *drowned* Persky—would have had to fly to Miami to change planes for Fort Myers before he could get to the island. From everything that followed, it's obvious that the man who eventually posed as Persky boarded the plane in Los Angeles along with the real Persky. They arrived at Miami International Airport with time to while away before Persky had to make his connection to Fory Myers, and that's where the false Persky did away with the real one.''

"By drowning him."

"Apparently."

"How did they end up at the bay?"

Greenfield uncrossed his legs and recrossed them in the other direction. "There's a canal right by the airport that, I believe empties into the Miami River. The river's nearby, in any case, and empties into the bay.'' (He'd been studying maps!) "Of course, if they had an hour or more between planes they could easily have rented a car and driven down to look at the ships. It's a sizable port.''

"And what? Conked him on the head and pushed him into the water?''

"Persky was a small man,'' I contributed, thinking of the slacks that weren't too long on me. At the look on Grafman's face, I added, "I believe.''

"He disposed of Persky,'' Greenfield said, "however he did it. He had the entire trip from Los Angeles to plan it. And presumably having lifted Persky's wallet and airline ticket before sending him into the bay, he went back to the airport and boarded the plane for Fort Myers, to retrieve the suitcase Persky had checked through in Los Angeles. According to Mrs. Rome, he didn't know Persky's bag by sight and had to check several luggage tags before he found it. She was at the neighboring carousel at the time.''

"Why take the bag? What's the point? What did he want it for?''

"He had to retrieve the bag, in order to establish that Persky had arrived in Fort Myers before disappearing. If the bag remained unclaimed, the search for Persky would lead back to Miami, and he obviously wouldn't want that. A disappearance from Fort Myers airport could keep the authorities searching fruitlessly for a long time.''

"So he picks up the bag.'' Grafman ground out his cigarillo. "Why didn't he get out of there? Why get mixed up with the rest of it?''

"Because he couldn't avoid *you*, Mr. Grafman.'' Greenfield

paused and gave Grafman a level look. "Because you were there to meet him."

"I was there to meet *Persky*. I didn't know this man. Never saw him before. He could've walked right by me. I didn't know Persky by sight either."

"Exactly. And if I were meeting someone at an airport and had no idea how to recognize him, I'd probably have him paged."

"Of *course* I had him paged."

"Of course. 'Mr. Alvin Persky, please come to the so-and so-Airlines desk.' If you were this man, what would *you* do, under the circumstances? In a state of tension. Not knowing whether or not this summons could be crucial to the outcome of the whole scheme. He went to the desk, of course, and walked right into your clutches. After that, he was forced to go through with the impersonation."

"Why didn't he just leave? Just say he'd changed his mind, didn't want the job? Had a better offer in New York?"

"And that wouldn't have made you suspicious or, at the very least, angry? The man knew that if he walked off for no good reason, you would be on the phone to Persky's California agent in a matter of minutes. And when Persky failed to show up back in Los Angeles within the next day or two, the hounds would be out and running, noses to the ground. No, he was stuck. He had to devise a way to leave as a logical result of a breakdown in negotiations. A failure that would be yours, not his. He was reasonably resourceful about it, too. First he invented laryngitis. After the discovery of the body, it escalated to the flu to escape questioning by the police. The initial laryngitis served to avoid having to talk on the phone with Persky's agent, or to discuss the play with you and Webber. In the first instance his voice would have given him away; in the second, his ignorance of the craft. I'm assuming he's not a writer. I'm damn sure he's not a writer." He stood up, went to the windows and looked down at the tacky bustle of Seventh Avenue. "Then he began to make unreasonable demands, designed to ensure an impasse that would force you to retract your offer. At which, naturally, he'd be free to leave without arousing suspicion. It wasn't an ideal situation, but once he was trapped, it was the best he could do. Unfortunately for him, Ruskin unexpectedly queered that ploy by capitulating to each demand. Finally, as our man saw it, his only recourse was to bring the whole project to an end by killing off its raison d'être: the woman for whom, I believe, you'd undertaken it in the first place."

Grafman looked away quickly, then stood up, went to a bookcase and stood with his back to us, fiddling with the books, pushing them around. "That's crazy," he said without turning. "He killed Thea because he wanted to get out of it? People don't *kill* for that kind of reason."

"He killed her because he had to hide the fact that he'd already killed Persky."

"He was an ordinary"—Grafman turned back into the room—"a nice, polite kid."

"Who doesn't consider a human life sacrosanct."

"What are you saying, the man's a psychotic?"

"That's a medical question. I'm not equipped to answer it. I don't know that psychopath is the word for him either. I'm not even certain the scale of moral priorities applies. Morality is a human concept, and I'm beginning to wonder if he belongs in that category."

"I was there," I said, "and there's nothing extraterrestrial about him."

"No. Unfortunately. He's our own native product." Greenfield went back to the armchair, sat down and stared at the worn rug. "He belongs to a breed of biped that seems to have multiplied here lately: looks like a man, functions like one, but has no visceral connection with the human race. He has very little use for the earth and what it produces, none at all for its people and its history. His heart, soul and brain are consecrated to the manipulation of esoteric machinery. His emotional and intellectual life is stirred only by the symbols of technological wizardry. He feels nothing at the sight of blood or tears, but agonizes over a crippled computer. He'd trade all of Daumier for one perfect electronic signal, all of Shakespeare for the right piece of software, all of Bach for the successor to the microchip. His species is quite popular these days. Someone like that"— he looked up from under his bushy gray eyebrows—"could become president."

Grafman picked up a script from the desk, slapped it down again. "Even if I *believe* this whole megillah, I don't hear you coming up with an explanation for what started the ball rolling, why he killed Persky in the first place."

"Mr. Grafman"—Greenfield leaned back and crossed his legs at the ankles—"how many reasons for murder have there been since the first tiller of the soil killed the first shepherd in a fit of jealousy because God, that day, decided He preferred meat to vegetables? Take your pick."

"Come on, that's a cop-out."

"If I had to put money on a motive," Greenfield said, "I'd say it had to be one of the only two things he considered important. The first, of course, is survival. Killing Miss Quinn was a matter of survival. The second would have to be inherent in his cardinal interest, and I've already told you what that is."

Grafman roamed around the room, pushing at things, picking them up, putting them down. His jaw clenched, he muttered, "The son of a bitch took me for a ride!" He picked up a pencil holder and slammed it back on the desk. Finally, "So what am I supposed to do with all this?"

Greenfield stood up. "I was hoping you might suggest to the authorities in Miami"—he moved to the door—"that they call Persky's agent in California and ask him to fly out to identify the body."

"And if the body isn't Persky?"

"Then I will owe Persky's agent the plane fare."

We left.

When the item appeared in the *Times,* I was in the downstairs office on Poplar Avenue, chatting with Helen and Calli. Greenfield's voice from the floor above summoned me and I went up the narrow stairway to his large, messy, floor-through room. He had folded the *Times* in thirds with the relevant column on top, and handed it to me. Section B, page four, column one, bottom of page, said that the body of a man washed up on Claughton Island in Biscayne Bay had been identified as that of

Alvin Persky of Los Angeles, a television writer whose credits included the popular weekly series *Barefoot*.

"Charlie? Do you think they'll get him for this one?"

"If they can find him."

CHAPTER EIGHTEEN

THEY FOUND HIM, FINALLY, SOME FORTY MILES FROM Sloan's Ford, in Manhattan, using a made-up name and social security number to work as an animator for a company that prided itself on producing "creative" television commercials. His legal name was Donald Marquette.

During the trial my mother forwarded every scrap of relevant news that appeared in the Lee County papers. Reading them, I thought Marquette's lawyers might have wished their client were a little less forthcoming under questioning: he seemed eager to impress the public with the fact that he was not a member of the lower orders, that he was part of the professional crew that kept the glamour world afloat.

Yes, he'd known Alvin Persky, they'd worked together some years ago for a West Coast advertising firm, Persky on copy, Marquette on graphics. They'd become friends as a result of their common interest in science fiction films. Eventually Persky had left advertising and gone on to become a successful writer for television.

How did he feel about Persky? They were fast friends. How

did he feel about Persky's success? It was all to the good, because, you see, Persky had come up with a fabulous adventure story, a story that lent itself to the use of dazzling technical tricks. On hearing the story, he, Marquette, had realized immediately its potential as a truly spectacular video game. It was revolutionary. It would sweep the country, maybe the world. And he, Marquette, knew exactly how to make it work, technically. It would make a fortune. Both he and Persky would leap to the top of the ladder. So, yes, he was happy about Persky's success: the closer Persky got to the sources of power and money, the better.

And what happened to that story? Well, Persky, unfortunately, was determined to peddle it as a large-screen feature. Marquette had spent many hours trying to dissuade him from that course. (Implication: the studios have their own technological geniuses and Marquette would be out in the cold.)

But Persky's agent said otherwise.

Had Marquette accompanied Persky on his flight to Miami? Yes. Why? To talk about the story. Why had he picked up Persky's bag at the Fort Myers airport? Well, he was looking for Persky. Persky had disappeared in Miami, so he'd taken the plane to Fort Myers hoping Persky would be there. And so on.

Grafman's testimony nailed it shut.

As usual before pronouncing sentence, the judge asked Marquette if he had anything to say. He certainly did.

"You see," he explained, seeming to feel this would clear up everything and alter the court's opinion of him, "Alvin wouldn't listen to me. He was preparing to give his agent a copy of the story to take around to the studios when he got this call from Mr. Grafman to come to the island. So I had no choice. I had to keep him from wasting that material. It was a story in a million. The perfect springboard for incredible feats of visual illusion. We would have created a technological miracle. It would have made video history. It would have become a classic. Legendary. I didn't do this for myself. I did it for science."

Yes, he said that. And then he played what he thought, apparently, was his ace.

"I'm the only one, now, who knows the story. I destroyed both copies."

Possibly he expected his words would have film moguls rushing to his aid, bringing their power to bear to arrange appeals, get the verdict reversed, in order to get their hands on this apotheosis of applied science.

Or perhaps he really believed the world would be on his side once they were able to see that technology must inevitably take precedence over human life.

GREENFIELD READ THIS FINAL ACCOUNT IN HIS OFFICE, SITTING at the Brobdingnagian desk that looked, with its customary clutter of papers, like an abandoned fairground.

"And all his technical sophistication, finally," he said, "was no use to him. When his future was at stake, he had to resort to a natural body of water, and a plant." He swung around to the desk, his swivel chair going through its variations on a chalk-and-blackboard theme. "If he ever goes down in the annals of crime, it will be as a monument to imperishable ignorance."

He picked up a blue pencil and Stewart's account of a local campaign to fight drunken driving by rolling back the bar-closing time, and went back to work.

He never again referred to the Sanibel episode, except to say "No!" when a year or so later, I mentioned noticing an announcement that a new Broadway musical called *Captiva*, Mitchell Grafman's name heading a block-long list of producers, would be having previews beginning the following week, and asked if he'd like to see it.

But I had gone back to Sanibel before that for a brief visit with Mother, who was doing ten laps a day in the pool and washing her hair twice a week. The Ruskins were again absent, having gone to New York, but this time there were strangers in their apartment.

I walked on the long white beach and, in the cool, quiet, lavender dawn, listened to the birds calling imperiously to each other as they swooped over the pepper trees and the red-tile roofs toward the Gulf. And before I left, I drove out to Captiva.

The track beside the gumbo-limbo was as corrugated as I remembered it, the tangled property on one side of it still unsold. The bicycle leaned against the side of the house. And Sarah

McChesney came shooting out of the front door to see who was invading her privacy.

We talked, we drank varnish tea, we toured the garden.

"That murderer," she said, "who's been in the papers, was right here, you know. On the island."

I nodded and finally asked the question I'd never been able to put to rest.

"Do you remember my asking you about Leroy? You said he was at the marina, the afternoon Thea disappeared. But that was his afternoon off. He wasn't there. Why did you say he was?"

The gray eyes grew large with indignation. "He was *there*! He was in the parking lot. In the back of a panel truck."

"In the *back*?"

She flicked hair out of her eyes. "With a silly little fat girl who helps out at the bike rental." She dismissed Leroy and looked out to the Gulf, speculating. "A murderer. On the island."

I left her carefully pruning an overgrown bush and singing to herself, a song Donald Marquette would never understand.

> *"What though on homely fare we dine,*
> *Wear hodden-gray an' a' that;*
> *Gie fools their silks, and knaves their wine*
> *A man's a man for a' that.*
> *For a' that, an'a'that,*
> *A man's a man for a' that . . ."*

ABOUT THE AUTHOR

Lucille Kallen has written for television (including the acclaimed series *Your Show of Shows*) and for the theater, and she is the author of the first feminist comic novel, *Outside There, Somewhere*. She began her mystery-writing career with INTRODUCING C.B. GREENFIELD, which was an American Book Award nominee, and followed with C.B. GREENFIELD: THE TANGLEWOOD MURDER and C.B. GREENFIELD: NO LADY IN THE HOUSE. Lucille Kallen is currently plotting the further adventures of C.B. Greenfield and Maggie Rome.